Cinderella:
The Ultimate Collection

Cinderella:
The Ultimate Collection

By

Brothers Grimm

Henry W. Hewet

Charles Perrault

Andrew Lang

Enhanced Media
2016

Cinderella: The Ultimate Collection.

Published by Enhanced Media.

Enhanced Media Publishing
Los Angeles, CA.

First Printing: 2016.

ISBN 978-1-365-11204-1

Cover image: *Cinderella* by John Everett Millais (1829 -1896).

Back: Andrew Lang (1844-1912).

Contents

The Cat Cinderella by Giambattista Basile

There was once a Prince who was a widower, and he had a daughter so dear to him that he saw with no other eyes but hers. He gave her an excellent teacher of sewing, who taught her chainwork, openwork, fringes and hems and showed her more love than was possible to describe. The father, however, shortly remarried, and his wife was an evil, malicious, bad-tempered woman who began at once to hate her step-daughter and threw sour looks, wry faces and scowling glances on her enough to make her jump with fright.

The poor child was always complaining to her governess of her step-mother's ill-treatment, finishing up with "O would to God that you could be my little mother, who are so kind and loving to me," and she so often repeated this song to her that she put a wasp in her ear and, at last, tempted by the devil, her teacher ended by saying, "If you must follow this madcap idea, I will be a mother to you and you shall be the apple of my eye." She was going on with the prologue, when Zezolla (as the girl was called) interrupted her by saying, "Forgive my taking the words out of your mouth. I know you love me well, mum's the word, and suffict; teach me the way, for I am new; you write and I will sign."

"Well, then," answered the governess, "listen carefully; keep your ears open and you shall always enjoy the whitest bread from the finest flour. When your father leaves the house, tell your step-mother that you would like one of those old dresses that are kept in the big chest in the closet, to save the one you now have on. As she always wants to see you in rags and tatters, she will open the chest and say, 'Hold the lid.' You must hold it while she is rummaging inside and then suddenly let it fall so that it breaks her neck. After that, you know well that your father would even coin false money to please you, so when he fondles you, beg him to take me for his wife, and then you shall be happy and the mistress even of my life."

When Zezolla had heard the plan, every hour seemed a thousand years until she had carried out her governess' advice in every particular. When the period of mourning for her step-mother was over, she began to sound her father about marrying the governess. At first the Prince took it as a joke, but Zezolla so often struck with the flat that at last she thrust with the point, and he gave way to the persuasive words of his daughter. Her therefore married Carmosina, the governess, with great celebrations.

Now while this couple were enjoying themselves, Zezolla was standing at a balcony of her house, when a dove flew on to the wall and said to her, "If ever you desire anything, send to ask for it from the dove of the fairies of the Island of Sardinia, and you will at once have it."

For five or six days the new step-mother lavished every sort of caress on Zezolla, making her take the best seat at table, giving her the best tidbits, and dressing her in the finest clothes. But after a little time the service that Zezolla had done her was forgotten, and banished from her memory (how sorry is the mind that has an evil mistress!) and she began to push forward six daughters of her own that she had kept in hiding till then, and so worked on her husband that they won his good graces and he let his own daughter slip out of his heart. So that, a loser today and a pauper tomorrow, Zezolla was finally brought to such a pass that she fell from the salon to the kitchen, from the canopy to the grate, from splendid silks and gold to dish-clouts, from sceptres to spits; not only did she change her state, but also her name, and was no longer called Zezolla, but "Cat Cinderella."

Now it happened that the Prince was forced to go to Sardinia on important affairs of State, and before he left he asked one by one of his step-daughters, Imperia, Colomba, Fiorella, Diamante, Colombina, and Pascarella, what they wanted him to bring back for them on his return. One asked for a splendid gown, another for a head-dress, one for cosmetics for the face, and another games to pass the time; one thing and one another. At last, and almost to make fun of her, he asked his daughter, "And you! what would you like?' and she answered, "Nothing, except to commend me to the dove of the fairies and beg them to send me something; and if you forget, may it be impossible for you to go forward or back. Bear in mind what I say: thy intent, thy reward."

The Prince went away, transacted his affairs in Sardinia, and bought the things his step-daughters had asked for, but Zezolla went quite out of his mind. But when they were embarked with the sails ready unfurled, it was found impossible to make the vessel leave the harbour: it seemed as if it were detained by a sea-lamprey. The captain of the ship, who was almost in despair, dropped off to sleep with weariness and in his dreams a fairy appeared to him who said, "Do you know why you cannot leave the harbour? Because the Prince who is with you has broken his promise to his daughter, remembering all the others except his own flesh and blood." As soon as he woke up the captain told his dream to the Prince, who was overcome with confusion at his omission. He went to the grotto of the fairies, and commending his daughter to them, begged that they should send her some gift.

Behold, out of the grotto there came a young girl, beautiful as a gonfalon, who bade him thank his daughter for her kind remembrances and tell

8

her to be of good cheer for love of her. With these words, she gave him a date tree, a spade and a golden can with a silken napkin; the date tree for planting and the other articles to keep and cultivate it.

The Prince, surprised at this present, took leave of the fairy and turned towards his own land. When he arrived, he gave his step-daughters the things they had asked for, and lastly he handed the fairy's present to his own daughter. Zezolla nearly jumped out of her skin with joy and planted the date tree in a fine pot, watering it every day and then drying it with the silken napkin.

As a result of these attentions, within four days the date tree grew to the size of a woman, and a fairy came out who said to the girl, "What do you want?" Zezolla answered that she would like sometimes to leave the house without the sisters knowing it. The fairy replied, "Whenever you want this, come to the plant and say:

O my golden date tree,
With golden spade, I've dug thee,
With golden can I've watered thee,
With golden napkin dried thee,
Strip thyself and robe thou me.

Then when you want to undress, change the last line and say: "Strip thou me and robe thou thee."

One day it happened to be a feast day, and the governess' daughters went out of the house in a procession all fluttering, bedaubed and painted, all ribbons, bells and gewgaws, all flowers and perfumes, roses and posies. Zezolla then ran to the plant and uttered the words the fairy had taught her, and at once she was decked out like a queen, seated on a white horse with twelve smartly attired pages. She too went where the sisters had gone, and though they did not recognize her, they felt their mouths water at the beauty of this lovely dove.

As luck would have it, the King came to this same place and was quite bewitched by the extraordinary loveliness of Zezolla. He ordered his most trusty attendant to find out about this fair creature, who she was and where she lived. The servant at once began to dog her footsteps, but she, noticing the trap, threw down a handful of crowns that she had obtained for that purpose from the date tree. The servant, fired by the desire for these glittering pieces, forgot to follow the palfrey and stopped to pick up the money, whilst she, at a bound, reached the house and quickly undressed in the way the fairy had told her. Those six harpies, her sisters, soon returned, and to vex and mortify her, described at length all the fine things that they had seen at the feast.

The servant in the meantime had returned to the King and had told him about the crowns, whereupon the King was furious, and angrily told him that he had sold his pleasure for a few paltry coins and that at the next feast he was at all costs to discover who this lovely girl was and where nested so fair a bird.

When the next feast-day came, the sisters went out, all bedecked and bedizened, leaving the despised Zezolla by the hearth. But she at once ran to the date tree and uttered the same words as before, and behold a band of maidens came out, one with the mirror and one with the flask of pumpkin water, one with the curling-tongs and another with the rouge, one with the comb and another with the pins, one with the dresses and one with the necklace and earrings. They all placed themselves round her and made her as beautiful as a sun and then mounted her in a coach with the six horses accompanied by footmen and pages in livery. She drove to the same place as before and kindled envy in the hearts of the sisters and flames in the breast of the King.

This time too, when she went away, the servant followed her, but so that he should not catch her up, she threw down a handful of pearls and jewels, which this trusty fellow was unable to resist pecking at, since they were not things to let slip. In this way Zezolla had time to reach home and undress herself as usual. The servant, quite stunned, went back to the King, who said, "By the soul of your departed, if you don't find that girl again, I'll give you a most thorough beating and as many kicks on your seat as you have hairs in your beard."

On the next feast-day, when the sisters had already started off, Zezolla went up to the date tree. She repeated the magic spell and was again magnificently dressed and placed in a golden coach with so many attendants around it that it looked as if she were a courtesan arrested in the public promenade and surrounded by police agents. After having excited the envy and wonder of her sisters, she left, followed by the King's servant, who this time fastened himself to the carriage by double thread. Zezolla, seeing that he was always at her side, cried, "Drive on," and the coach set off at such a gallop that in her agitation she let slip from her foot the richest and prettiest pattern you could imagine.

The servant, not being able to catch up to the carriage, which was now flying along, picked up the pattern and carried it to the King, telling him what had happened. The King took it in his hands and broke out into these words: "If the foundation is so fair, what must be the mansion? Oh, lovely candlestick which holds the candle that consumes me! Oh, tripod of the lovely cauldron in which my life is boiling! Oh, beauteous corks attached to the fishing-line of Love with which he has caught his soul! Behold, I embrace and enfold you, and if I cannot reach the plant, I worship the roots; if I cannot possess the capitals, I kiss the base: you first imprisoned a white foot, now you have ensnared a stricken heart. Through you, she who sways my life was taller by a span and a half; through you, my life grows by that much in sweetness so long as I keep you in my possession."

The King having said this called a secretary and ordered out the trumpeters and tantarara, and had it proclaimed that all the women in the land were to come to a festival and banquet which he had determined to give. On the appointed day, my goodness, what an eating and feasting there was! Where did all the tarts and cakes come from? Where all the stews and rissoles? All the macaroni and ravioli which were enough to stuff an entire army? The women were all there, of every kind and quality, of high degree and low degree, the rich and the poor, old and young, the well-favoured and the ill-favoured. When they had all thoroughly worked their jaws, the King spoke the proficiat and started to try the pattern on his guests, one by one, to see whom it fitted to a hair, so that he could find by the shape of the slipper the one whom he was seeking. But he could find no foot to fit it, so that he was on the point of despair.

Nevertheless, he ordered a general silence and said, "Come back tomorrow to fast with me, but as you love me well, do not leave behind a single woman, whoever she may be!" The Prince then said, "I have a daughter, but she always stays to mind the hearth, for she is a sorry, worthless creature, not fit to take her place at the table where you eat." The King answered, "Let her be at the top of the list, for such is my wish."

So they all went away, and came back the next day, and Zezolla came with Carmosina's daughters. As soon as the King saw her, he thought she was the one he wanted, but he hid his thoughts. After the banquet came the trial of the pattern. The moment it came near Zezolla's foot, it darted forward of itself to shoe that painted Lover's egg, as the iron flies to the magnet. The king then took Zezolla in his arms and led her to the canopy, where he put a crown on her head and ordered every one to make obeisance to her as to their queen. The sisters, livid with envy and unable to bear the torment of their breaking hearts, crept quietly home to their mother, confessing in spite of themselves that:

He is mad who would oppose the stars.

Cinderella, or The Little Glass Slipper by Charles Perrault

Once there was a gentleman who married, for his second wife, the proudest and most haughty woman that was ever seen. She had, by a former husband, two daughters of her own, who were, indeed, exactly like her in all things. He had likewise, by another wife, a young daughter, but of unparalleled goodness and sweetness of temper, which she took from her mother, who was the best creature in the world.

No sooner were the ceremonies of the wedding over but the stepmother began to show herself in her true colors. She could not bear the good qualities of this pretty girl, and the less because they made her own daughters appear the more odious. She employed her in the meanest work of the house. She scoured the dishes, tables, etc., and cleaned madam's chamber, and those of misses, her daughters. She slept in a sorry garret, on a wretched straw bed, while her sisters slept in fine rooms, with floors all inlaid, on beds of the very newest fashion, and where they had looking glasses so large that they could see themselves at their full length from head to foot.

The poor girl bore it all patiently, and dared not tell her father, who would have scolded her; for his wife governed him entirely. When she had done her work, she used to go to the chimney corner, and sit down there in the cinders and ashes, which caused her to be called Cinderwench. Only the younger sister, who was not so rude and uncivil as the older one, called her Cinderella. However, Cinderella, notwithstanding her coarse apparel, was a hundred times more beautiful than her sisters, although they were always dressed very richly.

It happened that the king's son gave a ball, and invited all persons of fashion to it. Our young misses were also invited, for they cut a very grand figure among those of quality. They were mightily delighted at this invitation, and wonderfully busy in selecting the gowns, petticoats, and hair dressing that would best become them. This was a new difficulty for Cinderella; for it was she who ironed her sister's linen and pleated their ruffles. They talked all day long of nothing but how they should be dressed.

"For my part," said the eldest, "I will wear my red velvet suit with French trimming."

"And I," said the youngest, "shall have my usual petticoat; but then, to make amends for that, I will put on my gold-flowered cloak, and my diamond stomacher, which is far from being the most ordinary one in the world."

They sent for the best hairdresser they could get to make up their head-pieces and adjust their hairdos, and they had their red brushes and patches from Mademoiselle de la Poche.

They also consulted Cinderella in all these matters, for she had excellent ideas, and her advice was always good. Indeed, she even offered her services to fix their hair, which they very willingly accepted. As she was doing this, they said to her, "Cinderella, would you not like to go to the ball?"

"Alas!" said she, "you only jeer me; it is not for such as I am to go to such a place."

"You are quite right," they replied. "It would make the people laugh to see a Cinderwench at a ball."

Anyone but Cinderella would have fixed their hair awry, but she was very good, and dressed them perfectly well. They were so excited that they hadn't eaten a thing for almost two days. Then they broke more than a dozen laces trying to have themselves laced up tightly enough to give them a fine slender shape. They were continually in front of their looking glass. At last the happy day came. They went to court, and Cinderella followed them with her eyes as long as she could. When she lost sight of them, she started to cry.

Her godmother, who saw her all in tears, asked her what was the matter.

"I wish I could. I wish I could." She was not able to speak the rest, being interrupted by her tears and sobbing.

This godmother of hers, who was a fairy, said to her, "You wish that you could go to the ball; is it not so?"

"Yes," cried Cinderella, with a great sigh.

"Well," said her godmother, "be but a good girl, and I will contrive that you shall go." Then she took her into her chamber, and said to her, "Run into the garden, and bring me a pumpkin."

Cinderella went immediately to gather the finest she could get, and brought it to her godmother, not being able to imagine how this pumpkin could help her go to the ball. Her godmother scooped out all the inside of it, leaving nothing but the rind. Having done this, she struck the pumpkin with her wand, and it was instantly turned into a fine coach, gilded all over with gold.

She then went to look into her mousetrap, where she found six mice, all alive, and ordered Cinderella to lift up a little the trapdoor. She gave each mouse, as it went out, a little tap with her wand, and the mouse was that moment turned into a fine horse, which altogether made a very fine set of six horses of a beautiful mouse colored dapple gray.

Being at a loss for a coachman, Cinderella said, "I will go and see if there is not a rat in the rat trap that we can turn into a coachman."

"You are right," replied her godmother, "Go and look."

Cinderella brought the trap to her, and in it there were three huge rats. The fairy chose the one which had the largest beard, touched him with her wand, and turned him into a fat, jolly coachman, who had the smartest whiskers that eyes ever beheld.

After that, she said to her, "Go again into the garden, and you will find six lizards behind the watering pot. Bring them to me."

She had no sooner done so but her godmother turned them into six footmen, who skipped up immediately behind the coach, with their liveries all bedaubed with gold and silver, and clung as close behind each other as if they had done nothing else their whole lives. The fairy then said to Cinderella, "Well, you see here an equipage fit to go to the ball with; are you not pleased with it?"

"Oh, yes," she cried; "but must I go in these nasty rags?"

Her godmother then touched her with her wand, and, at the same instant, her clothes turned into cloth of gold and silver, all beset with jewels. This done, she gave her a pair of glass slippers, the prettiest in the whole world. Being thus decked out, she got up into her coach; but her godmother, above all things, commanded her not to stay past midnight, telling her, at the same time, that if she stayed one moment longer, the coach would be a pumpkin again, her horses mice, her coachman a rat, her footmen lizards, and that her clothes would become just as they were before.

She promised her godmother to leave the ball before midnight; and then drove away, scarcely able to contain herself for joy. The king's son, who was told that a great princess, whom nobody knew, had arrived, ran out to receive her. He gave her his hand as she alighted from the coach, and led her into the hall, among all the company. There was immediately a profound silence. Everyone stopped dancing, and the violins ceased to play, so entranced was everyone with the singular beauties of the unknown newcomer.

Nothing was then heard but a confused noise of, "How beautiful she is! How beautiful she is!"

The king himself, old as he was, could not help watching her, and telling the queen softly that it was a long time since he had seen so beautiful and lovely a creature.

All the ladies were busied in considering her clothes and headdress, hoping to have some made next day after the same pattern, provided they could find such fine materials and as able hands to make them.

The king's son led her to the most honorable seat, and afterwards took her out to dance with him. She danced so very gracefully that they all more and more admired her. A fine meal was served up, but the young prince ate not a morsel, so intently was he busied in gazing on her.

She went and sat down by her sisters, showing them a thousand civilities, giving them part of the oranges and citrons which the prince had presented her with, which very much surprised them, for they did not know her. While Cinderella was thus amusing her sisters, she heard the clock strike eleven and three-quarters, whereupon she immediately made a courtesy to the company and hurried away as fast as she could.

Arriving home, she ran to seek out her godmother, and, after having thanked her, she said she could not but heartily wish she might go to the ball the next day as well, because the king's son had invited her.

As she was eagerly telling her godmother everything that had happened at the ball, her two sisters knocked at the door, which Cinderella ran and opened.

"You stayed such a long time!" she cried, gaping, rubbing her eyes and stretching herself as if she had been sleeping; she had not, however, had any manner of inclination to sleep while they were away from home.

"If you had been at the ball," said one of her sisters, "you would not have been tired with it. The finest princess was there, the most beautiful that mortal eyes have ever seen. She showed us a thousand civilities, and gave us oranges and citrons."

Cinderella seemed very indifferent in the matter. Indeed, she asked them the name of that princess; but they told her they did not know it, and that the king's son was very uneasy on her account and would give all the world to know who she was. At this Cinderella, smiling, replied, "She must, then, be very beautiful indeed; how happy you have been! Could not I see her? Ah, dear Charlotte, do lend me your yellow dress which you wear every day."

"Yes, to be sure!" cried Charlotte; "lend my clothes to such a dirty Cinderwench as you are! I should be such a fool."

Cinderella, indeed, well expected such an answer, and was very glad of the refusal; for she would have been sadly put to it, if her sister had lent her what she asked for jestingly.

The next day the two sisters were at the ball, and so was Cinderella, but dressed even more magnificently than before. The king's son was always by her, and never ceased his compliments and kind speeches to her. All this was so far from being tiresome to her, and, indeed, she quite forgot what her godmother had told her. She thought that it was no later than eleven when she counted the clock striking twelve. She jumped up and fled, as nimble as a deer. The prince followed, but could not overtake her. She left behind one of her glass slippers, which the prince picked up most carefully. She reached home, but quite out of breath, and in her nasty old clothes, having nothing left of all her finery but one of the little slippers, the mate to the one that she had dropped.

The guards at the palace gate were asked if they had not seen a princess go out. They replied that they had seen nobody leave but a young girl, very shabbily dressed, and who had more the air of a poor country wench than a gentlewoman.

When the two sisters returned from the ball Cinderella asked them if they had been well entertained, and if the fine lady had been there.

They told her, yes, but that she hurried away immediately when it struck twelve, and with so much haste that she dropped one of her little glass slippers, the prettiest in the world, which the king's son had picked up; that he had done nothing but look at her all the time at the ball, and that most certainly he was very much in love with the beautiful person who owned the glass slipper.

What they said was very true; for a few days later, the king's son had it proclaimed, by sound of trumpet, that he would marry her whose foot this slipper would just fit. They began to try it on the princesses, then the duchesses and all the court, but in vain; it was brought to the two sisters, who did all they possibly could to force their foot into the slipper, but they did not succeed.

Cinderella, who saw all this, and knew that it was her slipper, said to them, laughing, "Let me see if it will not fit me."

Her sisters burst out laughing, and began to banter with her. The gentleman who was sent to try the slipper looked earnestly at Cinderella, and, finding her very handsome, said that it was only just that she should try as well, and that he had orders to let everyone try.

He had Cinderella sit down, and, putting the slipper to her foot, he found that it went on very easily, fitting her as if it had been made of wax. Her two sisters were greatly astonished, but then even more so, when Cinderella pulled out of her pocket the other slipper, and put it on her other foot. Then in came her godmother and touched her wand to Cinderella's clothes, making them richer and more magnificent than any of those she had worn before.

And now her two sisters found her to be that fine, beautiful lady whom they had seen at the ball. They threw themselves at her feet to beg pardon for all the ill treatment they had made her undergo. Cinderella took them up, and, as she embraced them, said that she forgave them with all her heart, and wanted them always to love her.

She was taken to the young prince, dressed as she was. He thought she was more charming than before, and, a few days after, married her. Cinderella, who was no less good than beautiful, gave her two sisters lodgings in the palace, and that very same day matched them with two great lords of the court.

Moral: Beauty in a woman is a rare treasure that will always be admired. Graciousness, however, is priceless and of even greater value. This is what Cinderella's godmother gave to her when she taught her to behave like a queen. Young women, in the winning of a heart, graciousness is more important than a beautiful hairdo. It is a true gift of the fairies. Without it nothing is possible; with it, one can do anything.

Another moral: Without doubt it is a great advantage to have intelligence, courage, good breeding, and common sense. These, and similar talents come only from heaven, and it is good to have them. However, even these may fail to bring you success, without the blessing of a godfather or a godmother.

Aschenputtel by Jacob and Wilhelm Grimm

The wife of a rich man fell sick; and when she felt that her end drew nigh, she called her only daughter to her bed-side, and said, 'Always be a good girl, and I will look down from heaven and watch over you.' Soon afterwards she shut her eyes and died, and was buried in the garden; and the little girl went every day to her grave and wept, and was always good and kind to all about her. And the snow fell and spread a beautiful white covering over the grave; but by the time the spring came, and the sun had melted it away again, her father had married another wife. This new wife had two daughters of her own, that she brought home with her; they were fair in face but foul at heart, and it was now a sorry time for the poor little girl. 'What does the good-for-nothing want in the parlour?' said they; 'they who would eat bread should first earn it; away with the kitchen-maid!' Then they took away her fine clothes, and gave her an old grey frock to put on, and laughed at her, and turned her into the kitchen.

There she was forced to do hard work; to rise early before daylight, to bring the water, to make the fire, to cook and to wash. Besides that, the sisters plagued her in all sorts of ways, and laughed at her. In the evening when she was tired, she had no bed to lie down on, but was made to lie by the hearth among the ashes; and as this, of course, made her always dusty and dirty, they called her Ashputtel.

It happened once that the father was going to the fair, and asked his wife's daughters what he should bring them. 'Fine clothes,' said the first; 'Pearls and diamonds,' cried the second. 'Now, child,' said he to his own daughter, 'what will you have?' 'The first twig, dear father, that brushes against your hat when you turn your face to come homewards,' said she. Then he bought for the first two the fine clothes and pearls and diamonds they had asked for: and on his way home, as he rode through a green copse, a hazel twig brushed against him, and almost pushed off his hat: so he broke it off and brought it away; and when he got home he gave it to his daughter. Then she took it, and went to her mother's grave and planted it there; and cried so much that it was watered with her tears; and there it grew and became a fine tree. Three times every day she went to it and cried; and soon a little bird came and built its nest upon the tree, and talked with her, and watched over her, and brought her whatever she wished for.

Now it happened that the king of that land held a feast, which was to last three days; and out of those who came to it his son was to choose a bride for himself. Ashputtel's two sisters were asked to come; so they called her up, and said, 'Now, comb our hair, brush our shoes, and tie our sashes for us, for we are going to dance at the king's feast.' Then she did as she was told; but when all was done she could not help crying, for she thought to herself, she should so have liked to have gone with them to the ball; and at last she begged her mother very hard to let her go. 'You, Ashputtel!' said she; 'you who have nothing to wear, no clothes at all, and who cannot even dance—you want to go to the ball? And when she kept on begging, she said at last, to get rid of her, 'I will throw this dishful of peas into the ash-heap, and if in two hours' time you have picked them all out, you shall go to the feast too.'

Then she threw the peas down among the ashes, but the little maiden ran out at the back door into the garden, and cried out:

'Hither, hither, through the sky,
Turtle-doves and linnets, fly!
Blackbird, thrush, and chaffinch gay,
Hither, hither, haste away!
One and all come help me, quick!
Haste ye, haste ye!–pick, pick, pick!'

Then first came two white doves, flying in at the kitchen window; next came two turtle-doves; and after them came all the little birds under heaven, chirping and fluttering in: and they flew down into the ashes. And the little doves stooped their heads down and set to work, pick, pick, pick; and then the others began to pick, pick, pick: and among them all they soon picked out all the good grain, and put it into a dish but left the ashes. Long before the end of the hour the work was quite done, and all flew out again at the windows.

Then Ashputtel brought the dish to her mother, overjoyed at the thought that now she should go to the ball. But the mother said, 'No, no! you slut, you have no clothes, and cannot dance; you shall not go.' And when Ashputtel begged very hard to go, she said, 'If you can in one hour's time pick two of those dishes of peas out of the ashes, you shall go too.' And thus she thought she should at least get rid of her. So she shook two dishes of peas into the ashes.

But the little maiden went out into the garden at the back of the house, and cried out as before:

'Hither, hither, through the sky,
Turtle-doves and linnets, fly!
Blackbird, thrush, and chaffinch gay,
Hither, hither, haste away!
One and all come help me, quick!
Haste ye, haste ye!–pick, pick, pick!'

Then first came two white doves in at the kitchen window; next came
two turtle-doves; and after them came all the little birds under heaven, chirping and hopping about. And they flew down into the ashes; and the little
doves put their heads down and set to work, pick, pick, pick; and then the
others began pick, pick, pick; and they put all the good grain into the dishes,
and left all the ashes. Before half an hour's time all was done, and out they
flew again. And then Ashputtel took the dishes to her mother, rejoicing to
think that she should now go to the ball. But her mother said, 'It is all of no
use, you cannot go; you have no clothes, and cannot dance, and you would
only put us to shame': and off she went with her two daughters to the ball.
    Now when all were gone, and nobody left at home, Ashputtel went sor-
rowfully and sat down under the hazel-tree, and cried out:

'Shake, shake, hazel-tree,
Gold and silver over me!'

Then her friend the bird flew out of the tree, and brought a gold and
silver dress for her, and slippers of spangled silk; and she put them on, and
followed her sisters to the feast. But they did not know her, and thought it
must be some strange princess, she looked so fine and beautiful in her rich
clothes; and they never once thought of Ashputtel, taking it for granted that
she was safe at home in the dirt.
    The king's son soon came up to her, and took her by the hand and
danced with her, and no one else: and he never left her hand; but when anyone else came to ask her to dance, he said, 'This lady is dancing with me.'
    Thus they danced till a late hour of the night; and then she wanted to go
home: and the king's son said, 'I shall go and take care of you to your
home'; for he wanted to see where the beautiful maiden lived. But she
slipped away from him, unawares, and ran off towards home; and as the
prince followed her, she jumped up into the pigeon-house and shut the door.
Then he waited till her father came home, and told him that the unknown
maiden, who had been at the feast, had hid herself in the pigeon-house. But
when they had broken open the door they found no one within; and as they
came back into the house, Ashputtel was lying, as she always did, in her

dirty frock by the ashes, and her dim little lamp was burning in the chimney. For she had run as quickly as she could through the pigeon-house and on to the hazel-tree, and had there taken off her beautiful clothes, and put them beneath the tree, that the bird might carry them away, and had lain down again amid the ashes in her little grey frock.

The next day when the feast was again held, and her father, mother, and sisters were gone, Ashputtel went to the hazel-tree, and said:

'Shake, shake, hazel-tree,
Gold and silver over me!'

And the bird came and brought a still finer dress than the one she had worn the day before. And when she came in it to the ball, everyone wondered at her beauty: but the king's son, who was waiting for her, took her by the hand, and danced with her; and when anyone asked her to dance, he said as before, 'This lady is dancing with me.'

When night came she wanted to go home; and the king's son followed here as before, that he might see into what house she went: but she sprang away from him all at once into the garden behind her father's house. In this garden stood a fine large pear-tree full of ripe fruit; and Ashputtel, not knowing where to hide herself, jumped up into it without being seen. Then the king's son lost sight of her, and could not find out where she was gone, but waited till her father came home, and said to him, 'The unknown lady who danced with me has slipped away, and I think she must have sprung into the pear-tree.' The father thought to himself, 'Can it be Ashputtel?' So he had an axe brought; and they cut down the tree, but found no one upon it. And when they came back into the kitchen, there lay Ashputtel among the ashes; for she had slipped down on the other side of the tree, and carried her beautiful clothes back to the bird at the hazel-tree, and then put on her little grey frock.

The third day, when her father and mother and sisters were gone, she went again into the garden, and said:
'Shake, shake, hazel-tree,
Gold and silver over me!'
Then her kind friend the bird brought a dress still finer than the former one, and slippers which were all of gold: so that when she came to the feast no one knew what to say, for wonder at her beauty: and the king's son danced with nobody but her; and when anyone else asked her to dance, he said, 'This lady is my partner, sir.'

When night came she wanted to go home; and the king's son would go with her, and said to himself, 'I will not lose her this time'; but, however, she again slipped away from him, though in such a hurry that she dropped her left golden slipper upon the stairs.

The prince took the shoe, and went the next day to the king his father, and said, 'I will take for my wife the lady that this golden slipper fits.' Then both the sisters were overjoyed to hear it; for they had beautiful feet, and had no doubt that they could wear the golden slipper. The eldest went first into the room where the slipper was, and wanted to try it on, and the mother stood by. But her great toe could not go into it, and the shoe was altogether much too small for her. Then the mother gave her a knife, and said, 'Never mind, cut it off; when you are queen you will not care about toes; you will not want to walk.' So the silly girl cut off her great toe, and thus squeezed on the shoe, and went to the king's son. Then he took her for his bride, and set her beside him on his horse, and rode away with her homewards.

But on their way home they had to pass by the hazel-tree that Ashputtel had planted; and on the branch sat a little dove singing:

'Back again! back again! look to the shoe!
The shoe is too small, and not made for you!
Prince! prince! look again for thy bride,
For she's not the true one that sits by thy side.'

Then the prince got down and looked at her foot; and he saw, by the blood that streamed from it, what a trick she had played him. So he turned his horse round, and brought the false bride back to her home, and said, 'This is not the right bride; let the other sister try and put on the slipper.' Then she went into the room and got her foot into the shoe, all but the heel, which was too large. But her mother squeezed it in till the blood came, and took her to the king's son: and he set her as his bride by his side on his horse, and rode away with her.

But when they came to the hazel-tree the little dove sat there still, and sang:

'Back again! back again! look to the shoe!
The shoe is too small, and not made for you!
Prince! prince! look again for thy bride,
For she's not the true one that sits by thy side.'

Then he looked down, and saw that the blood streamed so much from the shoe, that her white stockings were quite red. So he turned his horse and brought her also back again. 'This is not the true bride,' said he to the father; 'have you no other daughters?' 'No,' said he; 'there is only a little dirty Ashputtel here, the child of my first wife; I am sure she cannot be the bride.' The prince told him to send her. But the mother said, 'No, no, she is much too dirty; she will not dare to show herself.' However, the prince would have her come; and she first washed her face and hands, and then went in and curtsied to him, and he reached her the golden slipper. Then she took her clumsy shoe off her left foot, and put on the golden slipper; and it fitted her as if it had been made for her. And when he drew near and looked at her face he knew her, and said, 'This is the right bride.' But the mother and both the sisters were frightened, and turned pale with anger as he took Ashputtel on his horse, and rode away with her. And when they came to the hazel-tree, the white dove sang:

'Home! home! look at the shoe!
Princess! the shoe was made for you!
Prince! prince! take home thy bride,
For she is the true one that sits by thy side!'

And when the dove had done its song, it came flying, and perched upon her right shoulder, and so went home with her.

The Baba Yaga by W. R. S. Ralston

ONCE upon a time there was an old couple. The husband lost his wife and married again. But he had a daughter by the first marriage, a young girl, and she found no favor in the eyes of her evil stepmother, who used to beat her, and consider how she could get her killed outright. One day the father went away somewhere or other, so the stepmother said to the girl, "Go to your aunt, my sister, and ask her for a needle and thread to make you a shift."

Now that aunt was a Baba Yaga. Well, the girl was no fool, so she went to a real aunt of hers first, and says she, "Good morning, auntie!"

"Good morning, my dear! What have you come for?"

"Mother has sent me to her sister, to ask for a needle and thread to make me a shift."

Then her aunt instructed her what to do. "There is a birch tree there, niece, which would hit you in the eye -- you must tie a ribbon round it; there are doors which would creak and bang -- you must pour oil on their hinges; there are dogs which would tear you in pieces -- you must throw them these rolls; there is a cat which would scratch your eyes out -- you must give it a piece of bacon."

So the girl went away, and walked and walked, till she came to the place. There stood a hut, and in it sat weaving the Baba Yaga, the bony-shanks.

"Good morning, auntie," says the girl.

"Good morning, my dear," replies the Baba Yaga.

"Mother has sent me to ask you for a needle and thread to make me a shift."

"Very well; sit down and weave a little in the meantime."

So the girl sat down behind the loom, and the Baba Yaga went outside, and said to her servant maid, "Go and heat the bath, and get my niece washed; and mind you look sharp after her. I want to breakfast off her."

Well, the girl sat there in such a fright that she was as much dead as alive. Presently she spoke imploringly to the servant maid, saying, "Kins-woman dear, do please wet the firewood instead of making it burn; and fetch the water for the bath in a sieve." And she made her a present of a handker-chief.

The Baba Yaga waited awhile; then she came to the window and asked, "Are you weaving, niece? Are you weaving, my dear?"

"Oh yes, dear aunt, I'm weaving."

So the Baba Yaga went away again, and the girl gave the cat a piece of bacon, and asked, "Is there no way of escaping from here?"

"Here's a comb for you and a towel," said the cat; "take them, and be off. The Baba Yaga will pursue you, but you must lay your ear on the ground, and when you hear that she is close at hand, first of all, throw down the towel. It will become a wide, wide river. And if the Baba Yaga gets across the river, and tries to catch you, then you must lay your ear on the ground again, and when you hear that she is close at hand, throw down the comb. It will become a dense, dense forest; through that she won't be able to force her way anyhow."

The girl took the towel and the comb and fled. The dogs would have rent her, but she threw them the rolls, and they let her go by; the doors would have begun to bang, but she poured oil on their hinges, and they let her pass through; the birch tree would have poked her eyes out, but she tied the ribbon around it, and it let her pass on. And the cat sat down to the loom, and worked away; muddled everything about, if it didn't do much weaving.

Up came the Baba Yaga to the window, and asked, "Are you weaving, niece? Are you weaving, my dear?"

"I'm weaving, dear aunt, I'm weaving," gruffly replied the cat.

The Baba Yaga rushed into the hut, saw that the girl was gone, and took to beating the cat, and abusing it for not having scratched the girl's eyes out. "Long as I've served you," said the cat, "you've never given me so much as a bone; but she gave me bacon." Then the Baba Yaga pounced upon the dogs, on the doors, on the birch tree, and on the servant maid, and set to work to abuse them all, and to knock them about.

Then the dogs said to her, "Long as we've served you, you've never so much as pitched us a burnt crust; but she gave us rolls to eat."

And the doors said, "Long as we've served you, you've never poured even a drop of water on our hinges; but she poured oil on us."

The birch tree said, "Long as I've served you, you've never tied a single thread around me; but she fastened a ribbon around me."

And the servant maid said, "Long as I've served you, you've never given me so much as a rag; but she gave me a handkerchief."

The Baba Yaga, bony of limb, quickly jumped into her mortar, sent it flying along with the pestle, sweeping away the while all traces of its flight with a broom, and set off in pursuit of the girl. Then the girl put her ear to the ground, and when she heard that the Baba Yaga was chasing her, and was now close at hand, she flung down the towel. And it became a wide, such a wide river! Up came the Baba Yaga to the river, and gnashed her teeth with spite; then she went home for her oxen, and drove them to the river. The oxen drank up every drop of the river, and then the Baba Yaga began the pursuit anew. But the girl put her ear to the ground again, and when she heard that the Baba Yaga was near, she flung down the comb, and instantly a forest sprang up, such an awfully thick one! The Baba Yaga began gnawing away at it, but however hard she worked, she couldn't gnaw her way through it, so she had to go back again.

But by this time the girl's father had returned home, and he asked, "Where's my daughter?"

"She's gone to her aunt's," replied her stepmother.

Soon afterwards the girl herself came running home.

"Where have you been?" asked her father.

"Ah, father!" she said, "mother sent me to aunt's to ask for a needle and thread to make me a shift. But aunt's a Baba Yaga, and she wanted to eat me!"

"And how did you get away, daughter?"

"Why like this," said the girl, and explained the whole matter.

As soon as her father had heard all about it, he became wroth with his wife, and shot her. But he and his daughter lived on and flourished, and everything went well with them.

The Little Glass Slipper by Henry W. Hewet

There once lived a gentleman and his wife, who were the parents of a lovely little daughter.

When this child was only nine years of age, her mother fell sick. Finding her death coming on, she called her child to her and said to her, "My child, always be good; bear every thing that happens to you with patience, and whatever evil and troubles you may suffer, you will be happy in the end if you are so." Then the poor lady died, and her daughter was full of great grief at the loss of a mother so good and kind.

The father too was unhappy, but he sought to get rid of his sorrow by marrying another wife, and he looked out for some prudent lady who might be a second mother to his child, and a companion to himself. His choice fell on a widow lady, of a proud and tyrannical temper, who had two daughters by a former marriage, both as haughty and bad-tempered as their mother. No sooner was the wedding over, than the step-mother began to show her bad temper. She could not bear her step-daughter's good qualities, that only showed up her daughters' unamiable ones still more obviously, and she accordingly compelled the poor girl to do all the drudgery of the household. It was she who washed the dishes, and scrubbed down the stairs, and polished the floors in my lady's chamber and in those of the two pert misses, her daughters; and while the latter slept on good feather beds in elegant rooms, furnished with full-length looking-glasses, their sister lay in a wretched garret on an old straw mattress. Yet the poor thing bore this ill treatment very meekly, and did not dare complain to her father, who thought so much of his wife that he would only have scolded her.

When her work was done, she used to sit in the chimney-corner amongst the cinders, which had caused the nickname of Cinderella to be given her by the family; yet, for all her shabby clothes, Cinderella was a hundred times prettier than her sisters, let them be dressed ever so magnificently.

The poor little Cinder-wench! this harsh stepmother was a sore trial to her; and how often, as she sate [sic] sadly by herself, did she feel that there is no mother like our own, the dear parent whose flesh and blood we are, and who bears all our little cares and sorrows tenderly as in the apple of her eye!

It happened that the king's son gave a ball, to which he invited all the nobility; and, as our two young ladies made a great figure in the world, they were included in the list of invitations. So they began to be very busy choosing what head-dress and which gown would be the most becoming. Here was fresh work for poor Cinderella: for it was she, forsooth, who was to starch and get up their ruffles, and iron all their fine linen; and nothing but dress was talked about for days together. "I," said the eldest, "shall put on my red velvet dress, with my point-lace trimmings." "And I," said the younger sister, "shall wear my usual petticoat, but shall set it off with my gold brocaded train and my circlet of diamonds."

They sent for a clever tire-woman to prepare the double rows of quilling for their caps, and they purchased a quantity of fashionably cut patches. They called in Cinderella to take her advice, as she had such good taste, and Cinderella not only advised them well, but offered to dress their hair, which they were pleased to accept. While she was thus busied, the sisters said to her: "And pray, Cinderella, would you like to go to the ball?"

"Nay, you are mocking me," replied the poor girl; "it is not for such as I to go to balls." "True enough," rejoined they; "folks would laugh to see a Cinderella at a court ball."

These two step-sisters were very cruel to Cinderella, and ill-used her much. Ah! what sweet friends are our own born sisters! there can be no substitutes like them in the whole wide world.

Any other but Cinderella would have dressed their hair awry to punish them for their impertinence, but she was so good-natured that she dressed them most becomingly. Although they disdained her, and while they would themselves make a great figure in the world, sought to degrade and lower her, see how the lovely disposition of Cinderella shines out. Although she was not allowed to go to the ball of the king's son, she not only advised them well how they could array themselves to appear to the best advantage, but she even what greatness of heart to do that! with her own hands dresses their hair, and in the most becoming manner her delicate taste can suggest.

The two sisters were so delighted, that they scarcely ate a morsel for a couple of days. They spent their whole time before a looking-glass, and they would be laced so tight, to make their waists as slender as possible, that more than a dozen stay-laces were broken in the attempt.

The long-wished-for evening came at last, and these proud misses stepped into the carriage and drove away to the palace. Cinderella looked after the coach as far as she could see, and then returned to the kitchen in tears; where, for the first time, she bewailed her hard and cruel degradation. She continued sobbing in the corner of the chimney, until a rapping at the kitchen-door roused her, and she got up to see what had occasioned, it. She found a little old beggar-woman hobbling on crutches, who besought her to give her some food. "I have only part of my own supper for you, Goody, which is no better than a dry crust. But if you like to step in and warm yourself, you can do so, and welcome." "Thank you, my dear," said the old woman in a feeble, croaking voice. She then hobbled in and took her seat by the fire.

"Hey! dearee me! what are all these tears, my child?" said the old woman. And then Cinderella told the old woman all her griefs; how her sisters had gone to the ball, and how she wished to go too, but had no clothes, or means to do so.

"But you shall go, my darling," said the old woman, "or I am not Queen of the Faeries or your Godmother. Dry up your tears like a good goddaughter and do as I bid you, and you shall have clothes and horses finer than any one."

Cinderella had heard her father often talk of her godmother, and tell her that she was one of those good faeries who protect children. Her spirits revived, and she wiped away her tears.

The faery took Cinderella by the hand, and said, "Now, my dear, go into the garden and fetch me a pumpkin." Cinderella bounded lightly to execute her commands, and returned with one of the finest and largest pumpkins she could meet with. It was as big as a beer barrel, and Cinderella trundled it into the kitchen, wondering what her godmother would do with it. Her godmother took the pumpkin, and scooped out the inside of it, leaving nothing but rind; she then struck it with her wand, and it instantly became one of the most elegant gilt carriages ever seen.

She next sent Cinderella into the pantry for the mouse-trap, bidding her bring six little mice alive which she would find in the trap. Cinderella hastened to the pantry, and there found the mice as the faery had said, which she brought to the old lady, who told her to lift up the door of the trap but a little way and very gently, so that only one of the mice might go out at a time.

Cinderella raised the mouse-trap door, and as the mice came out one by one, the old woman touched them with her wand, and transformed them into fine prancing dapple-gray carriage horses with long manes and tails, which were tied up with light-blue ribands.

"Now, my dear good child," said the faery, "here you have a coach and horses, much handsomer than your sisters', to say the least of them; but as we have neither a postilion nor a coachman to take care of them, run quickly to the stable, where the rat-trap is placed, and bring it to me."

Cinderella was full of joy, and did not lose a moment; and soon returned with the trap, in which there were two fine large rats. These, too, were touched with the wand, and immediately the one was changed into a smart postilion, and the other into a jolly-looking coachman in full finery.

Her godmother then said, "My dear Cinderella, you must go to the garden again before I can complete your equipage; when you get there, keep to the right side, and close to the wall you will see the watering-pot standing; look behind it, and there you will find six lizards, which you must bring to me immediately."

Cinderella hastened to the garden as she was desired, and found the six lizards, which she put into her apron and brought to the faery. Another touch of the wonderful wand soon converted them into six spruce footmen in dashing liveries, with powdered hair and pig-tails, three-cornered cocked hats and gold-headed canes, who immediately jumped up behind the carriage as nimbly as if they had been footmen and nothing else all their lives.

The coachman and postilion having likewise taken their places, the faery said to Cinderella, "Well, my dear girl, is not this as fine an equipage as you could desire to go to the ball with? Tell me, now, are you pleased with it?"

"O yes, dear godmother," replied Cinderella; and then, with a good deal of hesitation, added, "but how can I make my appearance among so many finely-dressed people in these mean-looking clothes?"

"Give yourself no uneasiness about that, my dear; the most laborious part of our task is already accomplished, and it will be hard if I cannot make your dress correspond with your coach and servants."

On saying this, the old woman, assuming her character of Queen of the Faeries, touched Cinderella with the magic wand, and her clothes were instantly changed into a most magnificent ball dress, ornamented with the most costly jewels. The faery took from her pocket a beautiful pair of elastic glass slippers, which she caused Cinderella to put on, and then desired her to get into the carriage with all expedition, as the ball had already commenced.

Two footmen opened the carriage door, and assisted the now beautifully dressed Cinderella into it. Her godmother, before she took leave, strictly charged her, on no account whatever to stay at the ball after the clock had struck twelve; and then added, that if she stopped but a single moment beyond that time, her fine coach, horses, coachman, postilion, and footmen, and fine apparel, would all return to their original shapes of pumpkin, mice, rats, lizards, and mean-looking clothes.

Cinderella promised faithfully to attend to every thing that the faery had mentioned; and then, quite overjoyed, gave the direction to the footman, who bawled out in a loud and commanding tone to the coachman, "To the Royal Palace." The coachman touched his prancing horses lightly with his whip, and swiftly the carriage started off, and in a short time reached the palace.

The arrival of so splendid an equipage as Cinderella's could not fail to attract general notice at the palace gates; and as it drove up to the marble portico, the servants in great numbers came out to see it. Information was quickly taken to the king's son, that a beautiful young lady, evidently some princess, was in waiting. His Royal Highness hastened to the door, welcomed Cinderella, and handed her out of the carriage. He then led her gracefully into the ball-room, and introduced her to his father, the king. The moment she appeared, all conversation was hushed, the violins ceased playing, and the dancing stopped short, so great was the sensation produced by the stranger's beauty. A confused murmur of admiration fluttered through the crowd, and each was fain to exclaim, "How surpassingly lovely she is!" The ladies were all busy examining her head-dress and her clothes, in order to get similar ones the very next day, if, indeed, they could meet with stuffs of such rich patterns, and find workwomen clever enough to make them up. "What a lovely creature! so fair! so beautiful! What a handsome figure! how elegantly she is dressed!" Even the prince's father, old as he was, could not behold her with indifference, but wiped his eye-glass and used it very much, and said very often to the queen, that he had never seen so sweet a being.

The king's son handed Cinderella to one of the most distinguished seats on the dais at the top of the Hall, and begged she would allow him to hand her some refreshments. Cinderella received them with great grace. When this was over, the prince requested to have the honour of dancing with her. Cinderella smiled consent; and the delighted prince immediately led her out to the head of the dance, just about to commence. The eyes of the whole company were fixed upon the beautiful pair.

The trumpets sounded and the music struck up, and the dance commenced; but if Cinderella's beauty, elegant figure, and the splendor of her dress, had before drawn the attention of the whole room, the astonishment at her dancing was still greater.

Gracefulness seemed to play in all her motions; the airy lightness with which she floated along as buoyant as thistle-down drew forth a general murmur of admiration. The hall rang with the loudest acclamations of applause, and the company, all in one voice, pronounced her the most elegant creature that had ever been seen. And this was the little girl who had passed a great part of her life in the kitchen, and had always been called a "Cinder-wench."

When the dance was ended, a magnificent feast was served up, consisting of all delicacies: so much was the young prince engaged with Cinderella, that he did not eat one morsel of the supper.

Cinderella drew near her sisters, and frequently spoke to them; and in her goodness of heart she offered them the delicacies which she had received from the prince: but they did not know she was their sister.

When Cinderella heard the clock strike three-quarters past eleven, she made a low courtesy to the whole assembly and retired in haste.

You see how fortune befriends the good-hearted, and even out of such unpromising material as a pumpkin and mice, can make a coach and six, with which to honor her worthy favorite. So Cinderella goes to the ball; but to teach her to be diligent and faithful in her engagements, her faery godmother enjoins upon her that she return home at twelve. Native beauty and grace attract the princely heart; and while the king's son pays no heed to her pretentious sisters, he is all grace and condescension to little Cinderella. Obedient to her engagement with her godmother, she returns in all the splendor and honor of the coach and six.

On reaching home, she found her godmother; and after thanking her for the treat she had enjoyed, she ventured to express a wish to return to the ball on the following evening, as the prince had requested her to do.

She was still relating to her godmother all that had happened at court, when her two sisters knocked at the door. Cinderella went and let them in, pretending to yawn and stretch herself, and rub her eyes, and saying, "How late you are!" just as if she was waked up out of a nap, though, truth to say, she had never felt less disposed to sleep in her life. "If you had been to the ball," said one of the sisters, "you would not have thought it late. There came the most beautiful princess ever seen, who loaded us with polite attentions, and gave us oranges and citrons."

Cinderella could scarcely contain her delight, and inquired the name of the princess. But they replied that nobody knew her name, and that the king's son was in great trouble about her, and would give the world to know who she could be. "Is she, then, so very beautiful?" said Cinderella, smiling. "Oh, my! how I should like to see her! Oh, do, my Lady Javotte, lend me the yellow dress you wear every day, that I may go to the ball and have a peep at this wonderful princess." "A likely story, indeed!" cried Javotte, tossing her head disdainfully, "that I should lend my clothes to a dirty Cinderella like you!"

Cinderella expected to be refused, and was not sorry for it, as she would have been puzzled what to do, had her sister really lent her the dress she begged to have.

On the following evening the sisters again went to the court ball, and so did Cinderella, dressed even more magnificently than before. The king's son never left her side, and kept paying her the most flattering attentions. The young lady was nothing loth to listen to him; so it came to pass that she forgot her godmother's injunctions, and, indeed, lost her reckoning so completely, that before she deemed it could be eleven o'clock, she was startled at hearing the first stroke of midnight. She rose hastily, and flew away like a startled fawn. The prince attempted to follow her, but she was too swift for him; only, as she flew she dropped one of her glass slippers, which he picked up very eagerly. Cinderella reached home quite out of breath, without either coach or footmen, and with only her shabby clothes on her back; nothing, in short, remained of her recent magnificence, save a little glass slipper, the fellow to the one she had lost.

The sentinels at the palace gate were closely questioned as to whether they had not seen a princess coming out; but they answered they had seen no one except a shabbily dressed girl, who appeared to be a peasant rather than a young lady.

On this second night, as you have taken notice, dazzled by worldly show and the pleasing flattery of her royal lover, Cinderella over-stays her time, and is compelled to make her way back to her father's house on foot and in rags an everlasting lesson to all the pretty little Cinderellas in the world to keep their word, and to act in good faith by such as befriend them. Never mind her heart is in the right place she is a charming good creature; and although virtue goes home in rags, it will leave some token behind some foot-print by which it can be known and traced wherever it has once walked. We shall hear from that little lost glass slipper again!

When the two sisters returned from the ball, Cinderella asked them whether they had been well entertained; and whether the beautiful lady was there? They replied, that she was; but that she had run away as soon as midnight had struck, and so quickly as to drop one of her dainty glass slippers, which the king's son had picked up, and was looking at most fondly during the remainder of the ball; indeed, it seemed beyond a doubt that he was deeply enamored of the beautiful creature to whom it belonged.

They spoke truly enough; for, a few days afterwards, the king's son caused a proclamation to be made, by sound of trumpet all over the kingdom, to the effect that he would marry her whose foot should be found to fit the slipper exactly. So the slipper was first tried on by all the princesses; then by all the duchesses; and next by all the persons belonging to the court; but in vain. It was then carried to the two sisters, who tried with all their might to force their feet into its delicate proportions, but with no better success. Cinderella, who was present, and recognized her slipper, now laughed, and said, "Suppose I were to try?" Her sisters ridiculed such an idea; but the gentleman who was appointed to try the slipper, having looked attentively at Cinderella, and perceived how beautiful she was, said that it was but fair she should do so, as he had orders to try it on every young maiden in the kingdom. Accordingly, having requested Cinderella to sit down, she no sooner put her little foot to the slipper, than she drew it on, and it fitted like wax. The sisters were quite amazed; but their astonishment increased tenfold when Cinderella drew the fellow slipper out of her pocket, and put it on. Her godmother then made her appearance; and, having touched Cinderella's clothes with her wand, made them still more magnificent than those she had previously worn.

Her two sisters now recognized her for the beautiful stranger they had seen at the ball; and, falling at her feet, implored her forgiveness for their unworthy treatment, and all the insults they had heaped upon her head. Cinderella raised them, saying, as she embraced them, that she not only forgave them with all her heart, but wished for their affection. She was then taken to the palace of the young prince, in whose eyes she appeared yet more lovely than before, and who married her shortly after.

Cinderella, who was as good as she was beautiful, allowed her sisters to lodge in the palace, and gave them in marriage, that same day, to two lords belonging to the court.

The amiable qualities of Cinderella were as conspicuous after as they had been before marriage.

This series of Fairy stories has for generations been listened to and read by Children with an inexpressible delight, which other books have failed to afford them.

The extravagance of the Stories the attractive manner of telling them the picturesque scenery described the marvellous deeds related the reward of virtue and punishment of vice, upon principles strictly in accordance with ethical laws, as applied to the formation of character, render them peculiarly adapted to induce children to acquire a love for reading, and to aid them to cultivate the affections, sympathies, fancy, and imagination.

The principle, that good examples only should be imitated, has been lost sight of in the Pictorial embellishment of these standard Fairy Stories, upon the assumption that indifferent pictures are good enough to give first impressions of Art to Children. If this holds true then language and morals of a questionable cast will subserve the same ends; but the fallacy of this dogma notwithstanding, no one upon reflection will deny.

That this edition of these Stories may be more perfect than any other extant, the publisher has embellished it with exquisite specimens of high Pictorial Art, from which Children may derive those correct ideas that will mature into the beautiful and grand.

Katie Woodencloak by Peter Christen Asbjørnsen and Jørgen Moe

Once on a time, there was a King who had become a widower. By his Queen he had one daughter, who was so clever and lovely, there wasn't a cleverer or lovelier Princess in all the world. So the King went on a long time sorrowing for the Queen, whom he had loved so much, but at last he got weary of living alone, and married another Queen, who was a widow, and had, too, an only daughter; but this daughter was just as bad and ugly as the other was kind, and clever, and lovely. The stepmother and her daughter were jealous of the Princess, because she was so lovely; but so long as the King was at home they daren't do her any harm, he was so fond of her.

Well, after a time he fell into war with another king, and went out to battle with his host, and then the stepmother thought she might do as she pleased; and so she both starved and beat the princess, and was after her in every hole and corner of the house. At last she thought everything too good for her, and turned her out to herd cattle. So there she went about with the cattle, and herded them in the woods and on the fells. As for food, she got little or none, and she grew thin and wan, and was always sobbing and sorrowful. Now in the herd there was a great dun bull, which always kept himself so neat and sleek, and often he came up to the princess, and let her pat him. So one day when she sat there, sad, and sobbing, and sorrowful, he came up to her and asked her outright why she was always in such grief. She answered nothing, but went on weeping.

"Ah!" said the bull, "I know all about it quite well, though you won't tell me; you weep because the queen is bad to you, and because she is ready to starve you to death. But food you've no need to fret about, for in my left ear lies a cloth, and when you take and spread it out, you may have as many dishes as you please."

So she did that, took the cloth and spread it out on the grass, and lo! it served up the nicest dishes one could wish to have; there was wine too, and mead, and sweet cake. Well, she soon got up her flesh again, and grew so plump, and rosy, and white, that the queen and her scrawny chip of a daughter turned blue and yellow for spite. The queen couldn't at all make out how her stepdaughter got to look so well on such bad fare, so she told one of her maids to go after her in the wood, and watch and see how it all was, for she thought some of the servants in the house must give her food. So the maid went after her, and watched in the wood, and then she saw how the step-daughter took the cloth out of the bull's ear, and spread it out, and how it served up the nicest dishes, which the stepdaughter ate and made good cheer over. All this the maid told the queen when she went home.

And now the king came home from war, and had won the fight against the other king with whom he went out to battle. So there was great joy throughout the palace, and no one was gladder than the king's daughter. But the queen shammed sick, and took to her bed, and paid the doctor a great fee to get him to say she could never be well again unless she had some of the dun bull's flesh to eat. Both the king's daughter and the folk in the palace asked the doctor if nothing else would help her, and prayed hard for the bull, for everyone was fond of him, and they all said there wasn't that bull's match in all the land. But no; he must and should be slaughtered, nothing else would do. When the king's daughter heard that, she got very sorrowful, and went down into the byre to the bull. There, too, he stood and hung down his head, and looked so downcast that she began to weep over him.

"What are you weeping for?" asked the bull.

So she told him how the king had come home again, and how the queen had shammed sick and got the doctor to say she could never be well and sound again unless she got some of the dun bull's flesh to eat, and so now he was to be slaughtered.

"If they get me killed first," said the bull, "they'll soon take your life too. Now, if you're of my mind, we'll just start off, and go away tonight."

"Well, the princess thought it bad, you may be sure, to go and leave her father, but she thought it still worse to be in the house with the queen; and so she gave her word to the bull to come to him.

At night, when all had gone to bed, the princess stole down to the byre to the bull, and so he took her on his back, and set off from the homestead as fast as ever he could. And when the folk got up at cockcrow next morning to slaughter the bull, why, he was gone; and when the king got up and asked for his daughter, she was gone too. He sent out messengers on all sides to hunt for them, and gave them out in all the parish churches; but there was no one who had caught a glimpse of them. Meanwhile, the bull went through many lands with the king's daughter on his back, and so one day they came to a great copper wood, where both the trees, and branches, and leaves, and flowers, and everything, were nothing but copper.

But before they went into the wood, the bull said to the king's daughter, "Now, when we get into this wood, mind you take care not to touch even a leaf of it, else it's all over both with me and you, for here dwells a troll with three heads who owns this wood."

No, bless her, she'd be sure to take care not to touch anything. Well, she was very careful, and leant this way and that to miss the boughs, and put them gently aside with her hands; but it was such a thick wood, 'twas scarce possible to get through; and so, with all her pains, somehow or other she tore off a leaf, which she held in her hand.

"AU! AU! what have you done now?" said the bull; "there's nothing for it now but to fight for life or death; but mind you keep the leaf safe."

Soon after they got to the end of the wood, and a troll with three heads came running up. "Who is this that touches my wood?" said the troll.

"It's just as much mine as yours," said the bull.

"Ah!" roared the troll, "we'll try a fall about that."

"As you choose," said the bull.

So they rushed at one another, and fought; and the bull he butted, and gored, and kicked with all his might and main; but the troll gave him as good as he brought, and it lasted the whole day before the bull got the mastery; and then he was so full of wounds, and so worn out, he could scarce lift a leg. Then they were forced to stay there a day to rest, and then the bull bade the king's daughter to take the horn of ointment which hung at the troll's belt, and rub him with it. Then he came to himself again, and the day after they trudged on again. So they traveled many, many days, until, after a long, long time, they came to a silver wood, where both the trees, and branches, and leaves, and flowers, and everything, were silvern.

Before the bull went into the wood, he said to the king's daughter, "Now, when we get into this wood, for heaven's sake mind you take good care; you mustn't touch anything, and not pluck off so much as one leaf, else it is all over both with me and you; for here is a troll with six heads who owns it, and him I don't think I should be able to master."

"No," said the king's daughter; "I'll take good care and not touch anything you don't wish me to touch."

But when they got into the wood, it was so close and thick, they could scarce get along. She was as careful as careful could be, and leant to this side and that to miss the boughs, and put them on one side with her hands, but every minute the branches struck her across the eyes, and, in spite of all her pains, it so happened she tore off a leaf.

"AU! AU! what have you done now?" said the bull. "There's nothing for it now but to fight for life and death, for this troll has six heads, and is twice as strong as the other, but mind you keep the leaf safe, and don't lose it."

Just as he said that, up came the troll. "Who is this," he said, "that touches my wood?"

"It's as much mine as yours," said the bull.

"That we'll try a fall about," roared the troll.

"As you choose," said the bull, and rushed at the troll, and gored out his eyes, and drove his horns right through his body, so that the entrails gushed out; but the troll was almost a match for him, and it lasted three whole days before the bull got the life gored out of him. But then he, too, was so weak and wretched, it was as much as he could do to stir a limb, and so full of wounds, that the blood streamed from him. So he said to the king's daughter she must take the horn of ointment that hung at the troll's belt, and rub him with it. Then she did that, and he came to himself; but they were forced to stay there a week to rest before the bull had strength enough to go on.

At last they set off again, but the bull was still poorly, and they went rather slow at first. So to spare time the king's daughter said as she was young and light of foot, she could very well walk, but she couldn't get leave to do that. No; she must seat herself up on his back again. So on they traveled through many lands a long time, and the king's daughter did not know in the least whither they went; but after a long, long time they came to a gold wood. It was so grand, the gold dropped from every twig, and all the trees, and boughs, and flowers, and leaves, were of pure gold. Here, too, the same thing happened as had happened in the silver wood and copper wood. The bull told the king's daughter she mustn't touch it for anything, for there was a troll with nine heads who owned it, and he was much bigger and stouter than both the others put together, and he didn't think he could get the better of him. No; she'd be sure to take heed not to touch it; that he might know very well. But when they got into the wood, it was far thicker and closer than the silver wood, and the deeper they went into it the worse it got. The wood went on getting thicker and thicker, and closer and closer; and at last she thought there was no way at all to get through it. She was in such an awful fright of plucking off anything, that she sat, and twisted and turned herself this way and that, and hither and thither, to keep clear of the boughs, and she put them on one side with her hands; but every moment the branches struck her across the eyes, so that she couldn't see what she was clutching at; and lo! before she knew how it came about, she had a gold apple in her hand. Then she was so bitterly sorry she burst into tears and wanted to throw it away; but the bull said she must keep it safe and watch it well, and comforted her as well as he could; but he thought it would be a hard tussle, and he doubted how it would go.

Just then up came the troll with the nine heads, and he was so ugly, the king's daughter scarcely dared to look at him. "Who is this that touches my wood?" he roared.

"It's just as much mine as yours," said the bull.

"That we'll try a fall about," roared the troll again.

"Just as you choose," said the bull; and so they rushed at one another, and fought, and it was such a dreadful sight the king's daughter was ready to swoon away. The bull gored out the troll's eyes, and drove his horns through and through his body, till the entrails came tumbling out; but the troll fought bravely; and when the bull got one head gored to death, the rest breathed life into it again, and so it lasted a whole week before the bull was able to get the life out of them all. But then he was utterly worn out and wretched. He couldn't stir a foot, and his body was all one wound. He couldn't so much as ask the king's daughter to take the horn of ointment which hung at the troll's belt, and rub it over him. But she did it all the same, and then he came to himself by little and little; but they had to lie there and rest three weeks before he was fit to go on again.

Then they set off at a snail's pace, for the bull said they had still a little farther to go, and so they crossed over many high hills and thick woods. So after a while they got upon the fells.

"Do you see anything?" asked the bull.

"No, I see nothing but the sky and the wild fell," said the king's daughter.

So when they climbed higher up, the fell got smoother, and they could see farther off.

"Do you see anything now?" asked the bull.

"Yes, I see a little castle far, far away," said the princess.

"That's not so little though," said the bull.

After a long, long time, they came to a great cairn, where there was a spur of the fell that stood sheer across the way.

"Do you see anything now?" asked the bull.

"Yes, now I see the castle close by," said the king's daughter, "and now it is much, much bigger."

"Thither you're to go," said the bull. "Right underneath the castle is a pigsty, where you are to dwell. When you come thither you'll find a wooden cloak, all made of strips of lath; that you must put on, and go up to the castle and say your name is Katie Woodencloak, and ask for a place. But before you go, you must take your penknife and cut my head off, and then you must flay me, and roll up the hide, and lay it under the wall of rock yonder, and under the hide you must lay the copper leaf, and the silvern leaf, and the golden apple. Yonder, up against the rock, stands a stick; and when you want anything, you've only got to knock on the wall of rock with that stick."

At first she wouldn't do anything of the kind; but when the bull said it was the only thanks he would have for what he had done for her, she couldn't help herself. So, however much it grieved her heart, she hacked and cut away with her knife at the big beast till she got both his head and his hide off, and then she laid the hide up under the wall of rock, and put the copper leaf, and the silvern leaf, and the golden apple inside it.

So when she had done that, she went over to the pigsty, but all the while she went she sobbed and wept. There she put on the wooden cloak, and so went up to the palace. When she came into the kitchen she begged for a place, and told them her name was Katie Woodencloak. Yes, the cook said she might have a place -- she might have leave to be there in the scullery, and wash up, for the lassie who did that work before had just gone away.

"But as soon as you get weary of being here, you'll go your way too, I'll be bound."

No; she was sure she wouldn't do that.

So there she was, behaving so well, and washing up so handily. The Sunday after there were to be strange guests at the palace, so Katie asked if she might have leave to carry up water for the prince's bath; but all the rest laughed at her, and said, "What should you do there? Do you think the prince will care to look at you, you who are such a fright?"

But she wouldn't give it up, and kept on begging and praying; and at last she got leave. So when she went up the stairs, her wooden cloak made such a clatter, the prince came out and asked, "Pray, who are you?"

"Oh, I was just going to bring up water for your Royal Highness's bath," said Katie.

"Do you think now," said the prince, "I'd have anything to do with the water you bring?" and with that he threw the water over her.

So she had to put up with that, but then she asked leave to go to church; well, she got that leave too, for the church lay close by. But first of all she went to the rock, and knocked on its face with the stick which stood there, just as the bull had said. And straightway out came a man, who said, "What's your will?"

So the princess said she had got leave to go to church and hear the priest preach, but she had no clothes to go in. So he brought out a kirtle, which was as bright as the copper wood, and she got a horse and saddle beside. Now, when she got to the church, she was so lovely and grand, all wondered who she could be, and scarce one of them listened to what the priest said, for they looked too much at her. As for the prince, he fell so deep in love with her, he didn't take his eyes off her for a single moment.

So, as she went out of church, the prince ran after her, and held the church door open for her; and so he got hold of one of her gloves, which was caught in the door. When she went away and mounted her horse, the prince went up to her again, and asked whence she came.

"Oh, I'm from Bath," said Katie; and while the prince took out the glove to give it to her, she said:

Bright before and dark behind,

Clouds come rolling on the wind;

That this prince may never see

Where my good steed goes with me.

The prince had never seen the like of that glove, and went about far and wide asking after the land whence the proud lady, who rode off without her glove, said she came; but there was no one who could tell where "Bath" lay.

Next Sunday someone had to go up to the prince with a towel.

"Oh, may I have leave to go up with it?" said Katie.

"What's the good of your going?" said the others; "you saw how it fared with you last time."

But Katie wouldn't give in; she kept on begging and praying, till she got leave; and then she ran up the stairs, so that her wooden cloak made a great clatter. Out came the prince, and when he saw it was Katie, he tore the towel out of her hand, and threw it into her face.

"Pack yourself off, you ugly troll," he cried; "do you think I'd have a towel which you have touched with your smutty fingers?"

After that the prince set off to church, and Katie begged for leave to go too. They all asked what business she had at church -- she who had nothing to put on but that wooden cloak, which was so black and ugly. But Katie said the priest was such a brave man to preach, what he said did her so much good; and so at last she got leave. Now she went again to the rock and knocked, and so out came the man, and gave her a kirtle far finer than the first one; it was all covered with silver, and it shone like the silver wood; and she got besides a noble steed, with a saddlecloth broidered with silver, and a silver bit.

So when the king's daughter got to the church, the folk were still standing about in the churchyard. And all wondered and wondered who she could be, and the prince was soon on the spot, and came and wished to hold her horse for her while she got off. But she jumped down, and said there was no need, for her horse was so well broke, it stood still when she bade it, and came when she called it.

So they all went into church, but there was scarce a soul that listened to what the priest said, for they looked at her a deal too much; and the prince fell still deeper in love than the first time.

When the sermon was over, and she went out of church. and was going to mount her horse, up came the prince again and asked her whence she came.

"Oh, I'm from Towelland," said the king's daughter; and as she said that, she dropped her riding whip, and when the prince stooped to pick it up, she said:

Bright before and dark behind,

Clouds come rolling on the wind;

That this prince may never see

Where my good steed goes with me.

So away she was again; and the prince couldn't tell what had become of her. He went about far and wide, asking after the land whence she said she came, but there was no one who could tell him where it lay; and so the prince had to make the best he could of it.

Next Sunday someone had to go up to the prince with a comb. Katie begged for leave to go up with it, but the others put her in mind how she had fared the last time, and scolded her for wishing to go before the prince -- such a black and ugly fright as she was in her wooden cloak. But she wouldn't leave off asking till they let her go up to the prince with his comb. So, when she came clattering up the stairs again, out came the prince, and took the comb, and threw it at her, and bade her be off as fast as she could. After that the prince went to church, and Katie begged for leave to go too. They asked again what business she had there, she who was so foul and black, and who had no clothes to show herself in. Might be the prince or someone else would see her, and then both she and all the others would smart for it; but Katie said they had something else to do than to look at her; and she wouldn't leave off begging and praying till they gave her leave to go.

So the same thing happened now as had happened twice before. She went to the rock and knocked with the stick, and then the man came out and gave her a kirtle which was far grander than either of the others. It was almost all pure gold, and studded with diamonds; and she got besides a noble steed, with a gold broidered saddlecloth and a golden bit.

Now when the king's daughter got to the church, there stood the priest and all the people in the churchyard waiting for her. Up came the prince running, and wanted to hold her horse, but she jumped off, and said, "No; thanks -- there's no need, for my horse is so well broke, it stands still when I bid him."

So they all hastened into church, and the priest got into the pulpit, but no one listened to a word he said; for they all looked too much at her, and wondered whence she came; and the prince, he was far deeper in love than either of the former times. He had no eyes, or ears, or sense for anything, but just to sit and stare at her.

So when the sermon was over, and the king's daughter was to go out of the church, the prince had got a firkin of pitch poured out in the porch, that he might come and help her over it; but she didn't care a bit -- she just put her foot right down into the midst of the pitch, and jumped across it; but then one of her golden shoes stuck fast in it, and as she got on her horse, up came the prince running out of the church, and asked whence she came.

"I'm from Combland," said Katie. But when the prince wanted to reach her the gold shoe, she said:

Bright before and dark behind,
Clouds come rolling on the wind;
That this prince may never see
Where my good steed goes with me.

So the prince couldn't tell still what had become of her, and he went about a weary time all over the world asking for "Combland," but when no one could tell him where it lay, he ordered it to be given out everywhere that he would wed the woman whose foot could fit the gold shoe.

So many came of all sorts from all sides, fair and ugly alike; but there was no one who had so small a foot as to be able to get on the gold shoe. And after a long, long time, who should come but Katie's wicked stepmother, and her daughter, too, and her the gold shoe fitted; but ugly she was, and so loathly she looked, the prince only kept his word sore against his will. Still they got ready the wedding feast, and she was dressed up and decked out as a bride; but as they rode to church, a little bird sat upon a tree and sang:

A bit off her heel,
And a bit off her toe;
Katie Woodencloak's tiny shoe
Is full of blood -- that's all I know.

And, sure enough, when they looked to it, the bird told the truth, for blood gushed out of the shoe.

Then all the maids and women who were about the palace had to go up to try on the shoe, but there was none of them whom it would fit at all.

"But where's Katie Woodencloak?" asked the prince, when all the rest had tried the shoe, for he understood the song of birds very well, and bore in mind what the little bird had said.

"Oh, she! think of that!" said the rest; it's no good her coming forward. "Why, she's legs like a horse."

"Very true, I daresay," said the prince; "but since all the others have tried, Katie may as well try too."

"Katie!" he bawled out through the door; and Katie came trampling up-stairs, and her wooden cloak clattered as if a whole regiment of dragoons were charging up.

"Now, you must try the shoe on, and be a princess, you too," said the other maids, and laughed and made game of her.

So Katie took up the shoe, and put her foot into it like nothing, and threw off her wooden cloak; and so there she stood in her gold kirtle, and it shone so that the sunbeams glistened from her; and, lo! on her other foot she had the fellow to the gold shoe.

So when the prince knew her again, he grew so glad, he ran up to her and threw his arms round her, and gave her a kiss; and when he heard she was a king's daughter, he got gladder still, and then came the wedding-feast; and so

Snip, snip, snover,
This story's over.

Tattercoats by Joseph Jacobs

IN a great palace by the sea there once dwelt a very rich old lord, who had neither wife nor children living, only one little granddaughter, whose face he had never seen in all her life. He hated her bitterly, because at her birth his favourite daughter died; and when the old nurse brought him the baby, he swore, that it might live or die as it liked, but he would never look on its face as long as it lived.

So he turned his back, and sat by his window looking out over the sea, and weeping great tears for his lost daughter, till his white hair and beard grew down over his shoulders and twined round his chair and crept into the chinks of the floor, and his tears, dropping on to the window-ledge, wore a channel through the stone, and ran away in a little river to the great sea. And, meanwhile, his granddaughter grew up with no one to care for her, or clothe her; only the old nurse, when no one was by, would sometimes give her a dish of scraps from the kitchen, or a torn petticoat from the rag-bag; while the other servants of the palace would drive her from the house with blows and mocking words, calling her 'Tattercoats', and pointing at her bare feet and shoulders, till she ran away crying, to hide among the bushes.

And so she grew up, with little to eat or wear, spending her days in the fields and lanes, with only the gooseherd for a companion, who would play to her so merrily on his little pipe, when she was hungry, or cold, or tired, that she forgot all her troubles, and fell to dancing, with his flock of noisy geese for partners.

But, one day, people told each other that the king was travelling through the land, and in the town nearby was to give a great ball, to all the lords and ladies of the country, when the prince, his only son, was to choose a wife.

One of the royal invitations was brought to the palace by the sea, and the servants carried it up to the old lord, who still sat by his window, wrapped in his long white hair and weeping into the little river that was fed by his tears.

But when he heard the king's command, he dried his eyes and bade them bring shears to cut him loose, for his hair had bound him a fast prisoner and he could not move. And then he sent them for rich clothes, and jewels, which he put on; and he ordered them to saddle the white horse, with gold and silk, that he might ride to meet the king.

Meanwhile Tattercoats had heard of the great doings in the town, and she sat by the kitchen door weeping because she could not go to see them. And when the old nurse heard her crying she went to the lord of the palace, and begged him to take his granddaughter with him to the king's ball.

But he only frowned and told her to be silent, while the servants laughed and said: 'Tattercoats is happy in her rags, playing with the gooseherd, let her be -- it is all she is fit for.'

A second, and then a third time, the old nurse begged him to let the girl go with him, but she was answered only by black looks and fierce words, till she was driven from the room by the jeering servants, with blows and mocking words.

Weeping over her ill success, the old nurse went to look for Tattercoats; but the girl had been turned from the door by the cook, and had run away to tell her friend the gooseherd how unhappy she was because she could not go to the king's ball.

But when the gooseherd had listened to her story, he bade her cheer up, and proposed that they should go together into the town to see the king, and all the fine things; and when she looked sorrowfully down at her rags and bare feet, he played a note or two upon his pipe, so gay and merry that she forgot all about her tears and her troubles, and before she well knew, the herdboy had taken her by the hand, and she, and he, and the geese before them, were dancing down the road towards the town.

Before they had gone very far, a handsome young man, splendidly dressed, rode up and stopped to ask the way to the castle where the king was staying; and when he found that they, too, were going thither, he got off his horse and walked beside them along the road.

The herdboy pulled out his pipe and played a low sweet tune, and the stranger looked again and again at Tattercoats' lovely face till he fell deeply in love with her, and begged her to marry him.

But she only laughed, and shook her golden head.

'You would be finely put to shame if you had a goosegirl for your wife!' said she; 'go and ask one of the great ladies you will see tonight at the king's ball, and do not flout poor Tattercoats.'

But the more she refused him the sweeter the pipe played, and the deeper the young man fell in love; till at last he begged her, as a proof of his sincerity, to come that night at twelve to the king's ball, just as she was, with the herdboy and his geese, and in her torn petticoat and bare feet, and he would dance with her before the king and the lords and ladies, and present her to them all, as his dear and honoured bride.

So when night came, and the hall in the castle was full of light and music, and the lords and ladies were dancing before the king, just as the clock struck twelve, Tattercoats and the herdboy, followed by his flock of noisy geese, entered at the great doors, and walked straight up the ballroom, while on either side the ladies whispered, the lords laughed, and the king seated at the far end stared in amazement.

But as they came in front of the throne, Tattercoats's lover rose from beside the king, and came to meet her. Taking her by the hand, he kissed her thrice before them all, and turned to the king.

'Father!' he said, for it was the prince himself, 'I have made my choice, and here is my bride, the loveliest girl in all the land, and the sweetest as well!'

Before he had finished speaking, the herdboy put his pipe to his lips and played a few low notes that sounded like a bird singing far off in the woods; and as he played, Tattercoats's rags were changed to shining robes sewn with glittering jewels, a golden crown lay upon her golden hair, and the flock of geese behind her became a crowd of dainty pages, bearing her long train.

And as the king rose to greet her as his daughter, the trumpets sounded loudly in honour of the new princess, and the people outside in the street said to each other:

'Ah! now the prince has chosen for his wife the loveliest girl in all the land!'

But the gooseherd was never seen again, and no one knew what became of him; while the old lord went home once more to his palace by the sea, for he could not stay at court, when he had sworn never to look on his grand-daughter's face.

So there he still sits by his window, if you could only see him, as you some day may, weeping more bitterly than ever, as he looks out over the sea.

Ashey Pelt by M. Damant

Well, my grandmother she told me that in them auld days a ewe might be your mother. It is a very lucky thing to have a black ewe.

A man married again, and his daughter, Ashey Pelt, was unhappy. She cried alone, and the black ewe came to her from under the greystone in the field and said, "Don't cry. Go and find a rod behind the stone and strike it three times, and whatever you want will come."

So she did as she was bid.

She wanted to go to a party. Dress and horses and all came to her, but she was bound to be back before twelve o'clock or all the enchantment would go, all she had would vanish.

The sisters they did na' like her, she was so pretty, and the stepmother she kept her in wretchedness just.

She was most lovely. At the party the prince fell in love with her, and she forgot to get back in time. In her speed a-running she dropped her silk slipper, and he sent and he went over all the country to find the lady it wad fit. When he came to Ashey Pelt's door he did not see her. The sisters was busy a-nipping and a-clipping at their feet to get on the silk slipper, for the king's son he had given out that he loved that lady sae weel he wad be married on whatever could fit on that slipper.

The sisters they drove Ashey Pelt out bye to be out of the road, and they bid her mind the cows. They pared down their feet till one o' them could just squeeze it on. But she was in the quare agony I'm telling you.

So off they rode away; but when he was passing the field the voice of the auld ewe cried on him to stop, and she says, says she:

Nippet foot, and clippet foot
Behind the king's son rides,
But bonny foot, and pretty foot
Is with the cathering hides.

So he rode back and found her among the cows, and he married her, and if they lived happy, so may you and me.

The Sharp Grey Sheep by J. F. Campbell

THERE was a king and a queen, and they had a daughter, and the queen found death, and the king married another. And the last queen was bad to the daughter of the first queen, and she used to beat her and put her out of the door. She sent her to herd the sheep, and was not giving her what should suffice her. And there was a sharp-horned grey sheep in the flock that was coming with meat to her.

The queen was taking wonder that she was keeping alive and that she was not getting meat enough from herself, and she told it to the henwife. The henwife thought that she would send her own daughter to watch how she was getting meat, and Ni Mhaol Charach, the henwife's daughter, went to herd the sheep with the queen's daughter. The sheep would not come to her so long as Ni Mhaol Charach was there, and Ni Mhaol Charach was staying all the day with her. The queen's daughter was longing for her meat, and she said-"Set thy head on my knee and I will dress thy hair." And Ni Mhaol Charach set her head on the knee of the queen's daughter, and she slept.

The sheep came with meat to the queen's daughter, but the eye that was in the back of the head of the bald black-skinned girl, the henwife's daughter, was open, and she saw all that went on, and when she awoke she went home and told it to her mother, and the henwife told it to the queen, and when the queen understood how the girl was getting meat, nothing at all would serve her but that the sheep should be killed.

The sheep came to the queen's daughter and said to her, "They are going to kill me, but steal thou my skin and gather my bones and roll them in my skin, and I will come alive again, and I will come to thee again."

The sheep was killed, and the queen's daughter stole her skin, and she gathered her bones and her hoofs and she rolled them in the skin; but she forgot the little hoofs. The sheep came alive again, but she was lame. She came to the king's daughter with a halting step, and she said, "Thou didst as I desired thee, but thou hast forgotten the little hoofs."

And she was keeping her in meat after that.

There was a young prince who was hunting and coming often past her, and he saw how pretty she was, and he asked, "Who's she?" And they told him, and he took love for her, and he was often coming the way; but the bald black-skinned girl, the henwife's daughter, took notice of him, and she told it to her mother, and the henwife told it to the queen.

The queen was wishful to get knowledge what man it was, and the henwife sought till she found out who he (was), and she told the queen. When the queen heard who it was she was wishful to send her own daughter in his way, and she brought in the first queen's daughter, and she sent her own daughter to herd in her place, and she was making the daughter of the first queen do the cooking and every service about the house.

The first queen's daughter was out a turn, and the prince met her, and he gave her a pair of golden shoes. And he was wishful to see her at the sermon, but her muime would not let her go there.

But when the rest would go she would make ready, and she would go after them, and she would sit where he might see her, but she would rise and go before the people would scatter, and she would be at the house and everything in order before her muime would come. But the third time she was there the prince was wishful to go with her, and he sat near to the door, and when she went he was keeping an eye on her, and he rose and went after her. She was running home, and she lost one of her shoes in the mud; and he got the shoe, and because he could not see her he said that the one who had the foot that would fit the shoe was the wife that would be his.

The queen was wishful that the shoe would fit her own daughter, and she put the daughter of the first queen in hiding, so that she should not be seen till she should try if the shoe should fit her own daughter.

When the prince came to try the shoe on her, her foot was too big, but she was very anxious that the shoe should fit her, and she spoke to the henwife about it. The henwife cut the points of her toes off that the shoe might fit her, and the shoe went on her when the points of the toes were cut.

When the wedding-day came the daughter of the first queen was set in hiding in a nook that was behind the fire.

When the people were all gathered together, a bird came to the window, and he cried, "The blood's in the shoe, and the pretty foot's in the nook at the back of the fire."

One of them said, "What is that creature saying?" And the queen said, "It's no matter what that creature is saying; it is but a nasty, beaky, lying creature." The bird came again to the window; and the third time he came, the prince said, "We will go and see what he is saying."

And he rose and he went out, and the bird cried, "The blood's in the shoe, and the pretty foot's in the nook that is at the back of the fire."

He returned in, and he ordered the nook at the back of the fire to be searched. And they searched it, and they found the first queen's daughter there, and the golden shoe on the one foot. They cleaned the blood out of the other shoe, and they tried it on her, and the shoe fit her, and so did the other one. The prince left the daughter of the last queen, and he married the daughter of the first queen, and he took her from them with him, and she was rich and lucky after that.

Rashin-Coatie by George B. Scott Douglas

ONCE, a long time ago, there was a gentleman had two lassies. The oldest was ugly and ill-natured, but the youngest was a bonnie lassie and good; but the ugly one was the favourite with her father and mother. So they ill-used the youngest in every way, and they sent her into the woods to herd cattle, and all the food she got was a little porridge and whey.

Well, amongst the cattle was a red calf, and one day it said to the lassie, "Gee that porridge and whey to the doggie, and come wi' me."

So the lassie followed the calf through the wood, and they came to a bonnie hoosie, where there was a nice dinner ready for them; and after they had feasted on everything nice they went back to the herding.

Every day the calf took the lassie away, and feasted her on dainties; and every day she grew bonnier. This disappointed the father and mother and the ugly sister. They expected that the rough usage she was getting would take away her beauty; and they watched and watched until they saw the calf take the lassie away to the feast. So they resolved to kill the calf; and not only that, but the lassie was to be compelled to kill him with an axe. Her ugly sister was to hold his head, and the lassie who loved him had to give the blow and kill him.

She could do nothing but greet; but the calf told her not to greet, but to do as he bade her; and his plan was that instead of coming down on his head she was to come down on the lassie's head who was holding him, and then she was to jump on his back and they would run off. Well, the day came for the calf to be killed, and everything was ready--the ugly lassie holding his head, and the bonnie lassie armed with the axe. So she raised the axe, and came down on the ugly sister's head; and in the confusion that took place she got on the calf's back and they ran away. And they ran and better nor ran till they came to a meadow where grew a great lot of rashes; and, as the lassie had not on many clothes, they pu'ed rashes, and made a coatie for her. And they set off again and travelled, and travelled, till they came to the king's house. They went in, and asked if they wanted a servant. The mistress said she wanted a kitchen lassie, and she would take Rashin-coatie. So Rashin-coatie said she would stop, if they keep it the calf too. They were willing to do that. So the lassie and the calf stoppit in the king's house, and everybody was well pleased with her; and when Yule came, they said she was to stop at home and make the dinner, while all the rest went to the kirk. After they were away the calf asked if she would like to go. She said she would, but she had no clothes, and she could not leave the dinner. The calf said he would give her clothes, and make the dinner too. He went out, and came back with a grand dress, all silk and satin, and such a nice pair of slippers. The lassie put on the dress, and before she left she said –

"Ilka peat gar anither burn,
An' ilka spit gar anither turn,
An' ilka pot gar anither play,
Till I come frae the kirk on gude Yule day."

So she went to the kirk, and nobody kent it was Rashin-coatie. They wondered who the bonnie lady could be; and, as soon as the young prince saw her, he fell in love with her, and resolved he would find out who she was, before she got home; but Rashin-coatie left before the rest, so that she might get home in time to take off her dress, and look after the dinner.

When the prince saw her leaving, he made for the door to stop her; but she jumped past him, and in the hurry lost one of her shoes. The prince kept the shoe, and Rashin-coatie got home all right, and the folk said the dinner was very nice.

Now the prince was resolved to find out who the bonnie lady was, and he sent a servant through all the land with the shoe. Every lady was to try it on, and the prince promised to marry the one it would fit. That servant went to a great many houses, but could not find a lady that the shoe would go on, it was so little and neat. At last he came to a henwife's house, and her daughter had little feet. At first the shoe would not go on, but she parted her feet, and slipped in her toes, until the shoes went on. Now the prince was very angry. He knew it was not the lady that he wanted; but, because he had promised to marry whoever the shoe fitted, he had to keep his promise.

The marriage day came, and, as they were all riding to the kirk, a little bird flew through the air, and it sang –

Clippit feet an' paret taes is on the saidle set;
But bonnie feet an' braw feet sits in the kitchen neuk.

"What's that ye say?" said the prince. "Oh," says the henwife, "would ye mind what a feel bird says?" But the prince said, "Sing that again, bonnie birdie." So the bird sings –

Clippit feet an' paret taes is on the saidle set;
But bonnie feet an' braw feet sits in the kitchen neuk."

The prince turned his horse and rode home, and went straight to his father's kitchen, and there sat Rashin-coatie. He kent her at once, she was so bonnie; and when she tried on the shoe it fitted her, and so the prince married Rashin-coatie, and they lived happy, and built a house for the red calf, who had been so kind to her.

Cap O'Rushes by Joseph Jacobs

WELL, there was once a very rich gentleman, and he'd three daughters, and he thought he'd see how fond they were of him. So he says to the first, "How much do you love me, my dear?"

"Why," says she, "as I love my life."

"That's good," says he.

So he says to the second, "How much do you love me, my dear?"

"Why," says she, "better nor all the world."

"That's good," says he.

So he says to the third, "How much do you love me, my dear?"

"Why, I love you as fresh meat loves salt," says she.

Well, he was that angry. "You don't love me at all," says he, "and in my house you stay no more." So he drove her out there and then, and shut the door in her face.

Well, she went away on and on till she came to a fen, and there she gathered a lot of rushes and made them into a kind of a sort of a cloak with a hood, to cover her from head to foot, and to hide her fine clothes. And then she went on and on till she came to a great house.

"Do you want a maid?" says she.

"No, we don't," said they.

"I haven't nowhere to go," says she; "and I ask no wages, and do any sort of work," says she.

"Well," says they, "if you like to wash the pots and scrape the sauce-pans you may stay," said they.

So she stayed there and washed the pots and scraped the saucepans and did all the dirty work. And because she gave no name they called her "Cap o' Rushes."

Well, one day there was to be a great dance a little way off, and the servants were allowed to go and look on at the grand people. Cap o' Rushes said she was too tired to go, so she stayed at home.

But when they were gone she offed with her cap o' rushes, and cleaned herself, and went to the dance. And no one there was so finely dressed as her.

Well, who should be there but her master's son, and what should he do but fall in love with her the minute he set eyes on her. He wouldn't dance with anyone else.

But before the dance was done Cap o' Rushes slipt off, and away she went home. And when the other maids came back she was pretending to be asleep with her cap o' rushes on.

Well, next morning they said to her, "You did miss a sight, Cap o' Rushes!"

"What was that?" says she.

"Why, the beautifullest lady you ever see, dressed right gay and ga'. The young master, he never took his eyes off her."

"Well, I should have liked to have seen her," says Cap o' Rushes.

"Well, there's to be another dance this evening, and perhaps she'll be there."

But, come the evening, Cap o' Rushes said she was too tired to go with them. Howsoever, when they were gone, she offed with her cap o' rushes and cleaned herself, and away she went to the dance.

The master's son had been reckoning on seeing her, and he danced with no one else, and never took his eyes off her. But, before the dance was over, she slipt off, and home she went, and when the maids came back she, pretended to be asleep with her cap o' rushes on.

Next day they said to her again, "Well, Cap o' Rushes, you should ha' been there to see the lady. There she was again, gay and ga', and the young master he never took his eyes off her."

"Well, there," says she, "I should ha' liked to ha' seen her."

"Well," says they, "there's a dance again this evening, and you must go with us, for she's sure to be there."

Well, come this evening, Cap o' Rushes said she was too tired to go, and do what they would she stayed at home. But when they were gone she offed with her cap o' rushes and cleaned herself, and away she went to the dance.

The master's son was rarely glad when he saw her. He danced with none but her and never took his eyes off her. When she wouldn't tell him her name, nor where she came from, he gave her a ring and told her if he didn't see her again he should die.

Well, before the dance was over, off she slipped, and home she went, and when the maids came home she was pretending to be asleep with her cap o' rushes on.

Well, next day they says to her, "There, Cap o' Rushes, you didn't come last night, and now you won't see the lady, for there's no more dances."

"Well I should have rarely liked to have seen her," says she.

The master's son he tried every way to find out where the lady was gone, but go where he might, and ask whom he might, he never heard anything about her. And he got worse and worse for the love of her till he had to keep his bed.

"Make some gruel for the young master," they said to the cook. "He's dying for the love of the lady." The cook she set about making it when Cap o' Rushes came in.

"What are you a-doing of?", says she.

"I'm going to make some gruel for the young master," says the cook, "for he's dying for love of the lady."

"Let me make it," says Cap o' Rushes.

Well, the cook wouldn't at first, but at last she said yes, and Cap o' Rushes made the gruel. And when she had made it she slipped the ring into it on the sly before the cook took it upstairs.

The young man he drank it and then he saw the ring at the bottom.

"Send for the cook," says he.

So up she comes.

"Who made this gruel here?" says he.

"I did," says the cook, for she was frightened.

And he looked at her,

"No, you didn't," says he. "Say who did it, and you shan't be harmed."

"Well, then, 'twas Cap o' Rushes," says she.

"Send Cap o' Rushes here," says he.

So Cap o' Rushes came.

"Did you make my gruel?" says he.

"Yes, I did," says she.

"Where did you get this ring?" says he.

"From him that gave it me," says she.

"Who are you, then?" says the young man.

"I'll show you," says she. And she offed with her cap o' rushes, and there she was in her beautiful clothes.

Well, the master's son he got well very soon, and they were to be married in a little time. It was to be a very grand wedding, and every one was asked far and near. And Cap o' Rushes' father was asked. But she never told anybody who she was.

But before the wedding she went to the cook, and says she:

"I want you to dress every dish without a mite o' salt."

"That'll be rare nasty," says the cook.

"That doesn't signify," says she.

"Very well," says the cook.

Well, the wedding-day came, and they were married. And after they were married all the company sat down to the dinner. When they began to eat the meat, that was so tasteless they couldn't eat it. But Cap o' Rushes' father he tried first one dish and then another, and then he burst out crying.

"What is the matter?" said the master's son to him.

"Oh!" says he, "I had a daughter. And I asked her how much she loved me. And she said 'As much as fresh meat loves salt.' And I turned her from my door, for I thought she didn't love me. And now I see she loved me best of all. And she may be dead for aught I know."

"No, father, here she is!" says Cap o' Rushes. And she goes up to him and puts her arms round him.

And so they were happy ever after.

The Hearth Cat by Consiglieri Pedroso

THERE was once a schoolmistress who was a widow, and had a daughter who was very plain. This mistress had a pupil who was very pretty, and the daughter of a traveller. The mistress was very attached to her father, and every day would beg the girl to ask him to marry her, promising to give her porridge made with honey. The girl went home to ask her father to marry her schoolmistress, as she would then give her porridge made with honey.

To this request the father replied that he would not marry her, for he well knew that though she said now that she would give her porridge made with honey, later on she would give her porridge with gall. Yet, as the child began to cry, begging her father to consent, the father, who loved his - child very much, in order to comfort her, replied that he would order a pair of boots to be made of iron, and hang them up until the boots would rust to pieces with age, when he would marry the mistress. The little girl, very pleased to hear this, went immediately to tell the mistress, who then instructed her pupil to wet the boots every day. The little girl did so, and after a while the boots fell to pieces, and she went and told her father of it.

He then said that he would marry the mistress, and on the following day' married her. So long as the father was at home the child was treated with kindness and affection, but the moment he went out the mistress was very unkind to her, and treated her badly. She one day sent her to graze a cow, and gave her a loaf, which she desired her to bring back whole, and an earthen pot with water, out of which she expected her to drink, and yet was to bring back full.

One day the mistress told the girl that she wished her to employ herself in winding some skeins of thread until the evening. The little girl went away crying and bewailing her lot; but the cow comforted her, and told her not to be distressed,- to fix the skein on her horns and unravel the thread. The good cow after that took out all the crumb from the loaf by making a small hole with one of her horns, and then stopped the aperture, and gave the girl the loaf back again entire. In the evening the girl returned home.

When her stepmother saw that she had finished her task, and brought all the thread ready wound, she was very vexed and wanted to beat her, saying that she was sure the cow had had something to do with it, and next day ordered the animal to be killed. At this the girl began to cry very bitterly, but the step-mother told her that she would have to clean and wash the cow's entrails in a tank they had, however grieved she might feel for the loss of the animal.

The cow, however, again told the girl not to be troubled, but to go and wash her entrails, but was to be careful to save whatever she saw come out of them. The girl did so, and when she was cleaning them she saw a ball of gold come out and fall into the water. The girl went into the tank to search for it, and there she saw a house with everything in it in disorder, and she began to arrange and make the house look tidy. She suddenly heard footsteps, and in her hurry she hid herself behind the door.

The fairies entered and began to look about, and a dog came in also with them, and went up to where she was and began to bark, saying: "Bow, bow, bow, behind the door hides somebody who did us good, and will yet render us more services. Bow, bow, bow, behind the door hides somebody who has done us good, and will yet render us more services."

The fairies, as they searched about, hearing the dog bark, discovered where the girl was hiding, and began to say to her, "We endow you by the power we possess with the gift of beauty, making you the most lovely maiden ever seen." The next fairy then said, "I cast a sweet spell over you, so that when you open your mouth to speak, pearls and gold shall drop from your lips." The third fairy coming forward said, "I endow you with every blessing, making you the happiest maiden in the world. Take the wand, it will grant you whatever you may ask."

The girl then left the enchanted region, and returned home, and as soon as the mistress's daughter saw her approach she commenced to cry out to her mother to come quickly and see the hearth-cat, who had come back at last. The mistress ran to greet her, and asked her where and what she had been doing all that time. The girl related the contrary of what she had seen, as the fairies had instructed her to do-that she had found a tidy house, and that she had disarranged everything in it, to make it look untidy. The mistress sent her own daughter there, and she had hardly arrived at the house when she began at once to do as her half-sister had told her; she disarranged everything, to make the house look untidy and uncared for. And when she heard the fairies coming in she hid behind the door.

The little dog saw her, and barking at her said, "Behind the door stands one who has done us much harm, and will still continue to molest us. Bow, bow, bow, behind the door stands one who has done us much harm, and will continue to molest us on the first opportunity." The fairies hearing this approached her, and one began to say, "I throw a spell over you which will render you the ugliest maid that can be found."

The next one took up the word and said, "I bewitch you, so that when you attempt to speak all manner of filth shall fall out of your mouth." And the third fairy said, "I also bewitch you, and you shall become the poorest and most wretched maid in existence." The mistress's daughter returned home, thinking she was looking quite a beauty; but when she came up close to her mother, and began to speak, the mother burst out crying on seeing her own daughter so disfigured and wretched. Full of rage, she sent her step-daughter to the kitchen, saying, that she was the hearth-cat, and that she should take care that she kept there, as the only place which was fit for her.

On a certain day the mistress and her daughter repaired to some races which were then taking place, but when the girl saw that they had left the house, she asked her divining rod to give her a very handsome dress, boots, a hat, and everything complete. She dressed and adorned herself with all she had, and went to the races, and stood in front of the royal stand. The mistress's daughter instantly saw her, and began to exclaim and cry out at the top of her voice, in the midst of all the people present, saying, "Oh! mother, mother, that beautiful maiden over there is our very hearth-cat."

The mother, to quiet her, told her to be calm; that the maiden was not her step-sister, as she had remained at home under lock and key. The races were hardly over when the girl departed home; but the king, who had seen her, was in love with her. The moment the mother reached home she asked the hearth-cat whether she had been out. She replied, that she had not; and showed her face besmeared with smut. Next day the girl asked the wand to strike and give her another dress which would be more splendid than the previous one. She put on her things and repaired to the races. The moment the king perceived her he felt very pleased indeed; but the races were hardly concluded than she retired in haste, and went into her carriage and drove home, leaving the king more in love than ever with her. The third day the girl asked the divining rod to give her .a garment which should surpass the other two in richness and beauty, and other shoes; and she went and attended the races. When the king saw her, he was delighted, but was again disappointed to see her depart before the races were concluded.

In her hurry to enter her carriage quickly, she let fall one of her slippers. The king picked it up and returned to the palace, and fell lovesick. The slipper had some letters upon it which said, "This shoe will only fit its owner."

The whole kingdom was searched to find the lady whose foot would be found to fit the slipper exactly, yet no one was found. The schoolmistress went to the palace to try the slipper on, but all her efforts were in vain. After her, her daughter followed, and endeavoured her best to fit the slipper on, but with no better success.

There only remained the hearth cat. The king inquired who was the next to try on the slipper, and asked the mistress if there was any other lady left in her house who could fit on the dipper. The schoolmistress then said that there only remained a hearth-cat in her house, but that she had never worn such a slipper. The king ordered the girl to be brought to the palace, and the mistress had no alternative but to do so. The king himself insisted on trying the slipper on the girl's foot, and the moment she put her little foot into the slipper and drew it on, it fitted exactly. The king then arranged that she should remain in the palace and married her. And he ordered the mistress and her daughter to be put to death.

Conkiajgharuna the Little Rag Girl by Marjory Wardrop

There was and there was not. There was a miserable peasant who had a wife and a little daughter. So poor was this peasant that his daughter was called Conkiajgharuna ('Little Rag Girl').

Some time passed, and his wife died. He was unhappy before, but now a greater misfortune had befallen him. He grieved and grieved, and at last he said to himself, "I will go and take another wife; she will mind the house, and tend my orphan child." So he arose and took a second wife, but this wife brought with her a daughter of her own. When this woman came into her husband's house and saw his child, she was angry in heart.

She treated Little Rag Girl badly. She petted her own daughter, but scolded her stepdaughter, and tried to get rid of her. Every day she gave her a piece of badly cooked bread, and sent her out to watch the cow, saying, "Here is a loaf; eat of it, give to every wayfarer, and bring the loaf home whole." The girl went, and felt very miserable.

Once she was sitting sadly in the field, and began to weep bitterly. The cow listened, and then opened its mouth, and said, "Why are you weeping? What troubles you?" The girl told her sad tale. The cow said, "In one of my horns is honey, and in the other is butter, which you can take if you want to, so why be unhappy?" The girl took the butter and the honey, and in a short time she grew plump. When the stepmother noticed this she did not know what to do for rage. She rose, and after that every day she gave her a basket of wool with her; this wool was to be spun and brought home in the evening finished. The stepmother wished to tire the girl out with toil, so that she should grow thin and ugly.

Once when Little Rag Girl was tending the cow, it ran away onto a roof. She pursued it, and wished to drive it back to the road, but she dropped her spindle on the roof. Looking inside she saw an old woman seated, and said to her, "Good mother, will you give me my spindle?"

The old dame replied, "I am not able, my child, come and take it yourself." The old woman was a devi.

The girl went in and was lifting up her spindle, when the old dame called out, "Daughter, daughter, come and look at my head a moment. I am almost eaten up."

The girl came and looked at her head. She was filled with horror; all the worms in the earth seemed to be crawling there. The little girl stroked her head and removed some, and then said, "You have a clean head. Why should I look at it?"

This conduct pleased the old woman very much, and she said, "When you leave here, go along such and such a road, and in a certain place you will see three springs -- one white, one black, and one yellow. Pass by the white and black, and put your head in the yellow and rinse it with your hands."

The girl did this. She went on her way, and came to the three springs. She passed by the white and black, and bathed her head with her hands in the yellow fountain. When she looked up she saw that her hair was quite golden, and her hands, too, shone like gold. In the evening, when she went home, her stepmother was filled with fury. After this she sent her own daughter with the cow. Perhaps the same good fortune would visit her!

So Little Rag Girl stayed at home while her stepsister drove out the cow. Once more the cow ran onto the roof. The girl pursued it, and her spindle fell down. She looked in, and seeing the devi woman, called out, "Dog of an old woman! Here! Come and give me my spindle!"

The old woman replied, "I am not able, child, come and take it yourself." When the girl came near, the old woman said, "Come, child, and look at my head."

The girl came and looked at her head, and cried out, "Ugh! What a horrid head you have! You are a disgusting old woman!"

The old woman said, "I thank you, my child; when you go on your way you will see a yellow, a white, and a black spring. Pass by the yellow and the white springs, and rinse your head with your hands in the black one."

The girl did this. She passed by the yellow and white springs, and bathed her head in the black once. When she looked at herself she was black as an African, and on her head there was a horn. She cut it off again and again, but it grew larger and larger.

She went home and complained to her mother, who was almost frenzied, but there was no help for it. Her mother said to herself, "This is all the cow's fault, so it shall be killed."

This cow knew the future. When it learned that it was to be killed, it went to Little Rag Girl and said, "When I am dead, gather my bones together and bury them in the earth. When you are in trouble come to my grave, and cry aloud, 'Bring my steed and my royal robes!'" Little Rag Girl did exactly as the cow had told her. When it was dead she took its bones and buried them in the earth.

After this, some time passed. One holiday the stepmother took her daughter, and they went to church. She placed a trough in front of Little Rag Girl, spread a large measure of millet in the courtyard, and said, "Before we come home from church fill this trough with tears, and gather up this millet, so that not one grain is left." Then they went to church.

Little Rag Girl sat down and began to weep. While she was crying a neighbor came in a said, "Why are you in tears? What is the matter?" The little girl told her tale. The woman brought all the brood hens and chicken, and they picked up every grain of millet, then she put a lump of salt in the trough and poured water over it. "There, child," said she, "there are your tears! Now go and enjoy yourself."

Little Rag Girl then thought of the cow. She went to its grave and called out, "Bring me my steed and my royal robes!" There appeared at once a horse and beautiful clothes. Little Rag Girl put on the garments, mounted the horse, and went to the church.

There all the folk began to stare at her. They were amazed at her grandeur. Her stepsister whispered to her mother when she saw her, "This girl is very much like our Little Rag Girl!"

Her mother smiled scornfully and said, "Who would give that sun darkener such robes?"

Little Rag Girl left the church before anyone else; she changed her clothes in time to appear before her stepmother in rags. On the way home, as she was leaping over a stream, in her haste she let her slipper fall in.

A long time passed. Once when the king's horses were drinking water in this stream, they saw the shining slipper and were so afraid that they would drink no more water. The king was told that there was something shining in the stream, and that the horses were afraid.

The king commanded his divers to find out what it was. They found the golden slipper, and presented it to the king. When he saw it, he commanded his viziers, saying, "Go and seek the owner of this slipper, for I will wed none but her." His viziers sought the maiden, but they could find no one whom the slipper would fit.

Little Rag Girl's mother heard this, adorned her daughter, and placed her on a throne. Then she went and told the king that she had a daughter whose foot he might look at. It was exactly the model for the shoe. She put Little Rag Girl in a corner, with a big basket over her. When the king came into the house he sat down on the basket, in order to try on the slipper.

Little Rag Girl took a needle and pricked the king from under the basket. He jumped up, stinging with pain, and asked the stepmother what she had under the basket. The stepmother replied, "It is only a turkey I have there."

The king sat down on the basket again, and Little Rag Girl again stuck the needle into him. The king jumped up, and cried out, "Lift the basket. I will see underneath!"

The stepmother pleaded with him, saying, "Do not blame me, your majesty, it is only a turkey, and it will run away."

But the king would not listen to her pleas. He lifted the basket up, and Little Rag Girl came forth, and said, "This slipper is mine, and fits me well." She sat down, and the king found that it was indeed a perfect fit. Little Rag Girl became the king's wife, and her shameless stepmother was left with a dry throat.

Pepelyouga by Woislave M. Petrovitch

On a high pasture land, near an immense precipice, some maidens were occupied in spinning and attending to their grazing cattle, when an old strange looking man with a white beard reaching down to his girdle approached, and said, "Oh fair maidens, beware of the abyss, for if one of you should drop her spindle down the cliff, her mother would be turned into a cow that very moment."

So saying the aged man disappeared, and the girls, bewildered by his words, and discussing the strange incident, approached near to the ravine which had suddenly become interesting to them. They peered curiously over the edge, as though expecting to see some unaccustomed sight, when suddenly the most beautiful of the maidens let her spindle drop from her hand, and before she could recover it, it was bounding from rock to rock into the depths beneath. When she returned home that evening she found her worst fears realized, for her mother stood before the door transformed into a cow.

A short time later her father married again. His new wife was a widow, and brought a daughter of her own into her new home. This girl was not particularly well favored, and her mother immediately began to hate her stepdaughter because of the latter's good looks. She forbade her henceforth to wash her face, to comb her hair or to change her clothes, and in every way she could think of she sought to make her miserable.

One morning she gave her a bag filled with hemp, saying, "If you do not spin this and make a fine top of it by tonight, you need not return home, for I intend to kill you."

The poor girl, deeply dejected, walked behind the cattle, industriously spinning as she went, but by noon when the cattle lay down in the shade to rest, she observed that she had made but little progress and she began to weep bitterly.

Now, her mother was driven daily to pasture with the other cows, and seeing her daughter's tears she drew near and asked why she wept, whereupon the maiden told her all. Then the cow comforted her daughter, saying, "My darling child, be consoled! Let me take the hemp into my mouth and chew it; through my ear a thread will come out. You must take the end of this and wind it into a top." So this was done; the hemp was soon spun, and when the girl gave it to her stepmother that evening, she was greatly surprised.

Next morning the woman roughly ordered the maiden to spin a still larger bag of hemp, and as the girl, thanks to her mother, spun and wound it all, her stepmother, on the following day, gave her twice the quantity to spin. Nevertheless, the girl brought home at night even that unusually large quantity well spun, and her stepmother concluded that the poor girl was not spinning alone, but that other maidens, her friends, were giving her help. Therefore she, next morning, sent her own daughter to spy upon the poor girl and to report what she saw. The girl soon noticed that the cow helped the poor orphan by chewing the hemp, while she drew the thread and wound it on a top, and she ran back home and informed her mother of what she had seen. Upon this, the stepmother insisted that her husband should order that particular cow to be slaughtered. Her husband at first hesitated, but as his wife urged him more and more, he finally decided to do as she wished.

On learning what had been decided, the stepdaughter wept more than ever, and when her mother asked what was the matter, she told her tearfully all that had been arranged. Thereupon the cow said to her daughter, "Wipe away your tears, and do not cry any more. When they slaughter me, you must take great care not to eat any of the meat, but after the repast, carefully collect my bones and inter them behind the house under a certain stone; then, should you ever be in need of help, come to my grave and there you will find it."

The cow was killed, and when the meat was served the poor girl declined to eat of it, pretending that she had no appetite; after the meal she gathered with great care all the bones and buried them on the spot indicated by her mother.

Now, the name of the maiden was Marra, but, as she had to do the roughest work of the house, such as carrying water, washing, and sweeping, she was called by her stepmother and stepsister Pepelyouga (Cinderella).

One Sunday, when the stepmother and her daughter had dressed themselves for church, the woman spread about the house the contents of a basketful of millet, and said, "Listen, Pepelyouga; if you do not gather up all this millet and have dinner ready by the time we return from church, I will kill you!"

When they had gone, the poor girl began to weep, reflecting, "As to the dinner I can easily prepare it, but how can I possibly gather up all this millet?" But that very moment she recalled the words of the cow, that, if she ever should be struck by misfortune, she need but walk to the grave behind the house, when she would find instant help there. Immediately she ran out, and, when she approached the grave, lo! a chest was lying on the grave wide open, and inside were beautiful dresses and everything necessary for a lady's toilet. Two doves were sitting on the lid of the chest, and as the girl drew near, they said to her, "Marra, take from the chest the dress you like the best, clothe yourself, and go to church. As to the millet and other work, we ourselves will attend to that and see that everything is in good order!"

Marra needed no second invitation; she took the first silk dress she touched, made her toilet, and went to church, where her entrance created quite a sensation. Everybody, men and women, greatly admired her beauty and her costly attire, but they were puzzled as to who she was, and where she came from. A prince happened to be in the church on that day, and he, too, admired the beautiful maiden.

Just before the service ended, the girl stole from the church, went hurriedly home, took off her beautiful clothes and placed them back in the chest, which instantly shut and became invisible. She then rushed to the kitchen, where she discovered that the dinner was quite ready, and that the millet was gathered into the basket. Soon the stepmother came back with her daughter, and they were astounded to find the millet gathered up, dinner prepared, and everything else in order. A desire to learn the secret now began to torment the stepmother mightily.

Next Sunday everything happened as before, except that the girl found in the chest a silver dress, and that the prince felt a greater admiration for her, so much so that he was unable, even for a moment to take his eyes from her. On the third Sunday, the mother and daughter again prepared to go to church, and, having scattered the millet as before, she repeated her previous threats. As soon as they disappeared, the girl ran straight to her mother's grave, where she found, as on the previous occasions, the open chest and the same two doves. This time she found a dress made of gold lace, and she hastily clad herself in it and went to church, where she was admired by all, even more than before. As for the czar's son, he had come with the intention not to let her this time out of his sight, but to follow and see where she went. Accordingly, as the service drew near to its close, and the maiden withdrew quietly as before, the enamored prince followed after her. Marra hurried along, for she had none too much time, and, as she went, one of her golden slippers came off, and she was too agitated to stop and pick it up. The prince, however, who had lost sight of the maiden, saw the slipper and put it in his pocket. Reaching home, Marra took off her golden dress, laid it in the chest, and rushed back to the house.

The prince now resolved to go from house to house throughout his father's realm in search of the owner of the slipper, inviting all the fair maidens to try on the golden slipper. But, alas! his efforts seemed to be doomed to failure; for some girls the slipper was too long, for others too short, for others, again, too narrow. There was no one whom it would fit.

Wandering from door to door, the sad prince at length came to the house of Marra's father. The stepmother was expecting him, and she had hidden her stepdaughter under a large trough in the courtyard. When the prince asked whether she had any daughters, the stepmother answered that she had but one, and she presented the girl to him. The prince requested the girl to try on the slipper, but, squeeze as she would, there was not room in it even for her toes! Thereupon the prince asked whether it was true that there were no other girls in the house, and the stepmother replied that indeed it was quite true.

That very moment a cock flew onto the trough and crowed out lustily, "Kook-oo-ryeh-koooo! Here she is under this very trough!"

The stepmother, enraged, exclaimed, "Sh! Go away! May an eagle seize you and fly off with you!" The curiosity of the prince was aroused. He approached the trough, lifted it up, and, to his great surprise, there was the maiden whom he had seen three times in church, clad in the very same golden dress she had last worn, and having only one golden slipper.

When the prince recognized the maiden he was overcome with joy. Quickly he tried the slipper on her dainty foot. It not only fit her admirably, but it exactly matched the one she already wore on her left foot. He lifted her up tenderly and escorted her to his palace. Later he won her love, and they were happily married.

The Wonderful Birch by Andrew Lang

ONCE upon a time there were a man and a woman, who had an only daughter. Now it happened that one of their sheep went astray, and they set out to look for it, and searched and searched, each in n different part of the wood. Then the good wife met a witch, who said to her, "If you spit, you miserable creature, if you spit into the sheath of my knife, or if you run between my legs, I shall change you into a black sheep."

The woman neither spat, nor did she run between her legs, but yet the witch changed her into a sheep. Then she made herself look exactly like the woman, and called out to the good man, "Ho, old man, halloa! I have found the sheep already!"

The man thought the witch was really his wife, and he did not know that his wife was the sheep; so he went home with her, glad at heart because his sheep was found. When they were safe at home the witch said to the man, "Look here, old man, we must really kill that sheep lest it run away to the wood again."

The man, who was a peaceable quiet sort of fellow, made no objections, but simply said, "Good, let us do so."

The daughter, however, had overheard their talk, and she ran to the flock and lamented aloud, "Oh, dear little mother, they are going to slaughter you!"

"Well, then, if they do slaughter me," was the black sheep's answer, "eat you neither the meat nor the broth that is made of me, but gather all my bones, and bury them by the edge of the field."

Shortly after this they took the black sheep from the flock and slaughtered it. The witch made pease-soup of it, and set it before the daughter. But the girl remembered her mother's warning.

She did not touch the soup, but she carried the bones to the edge of the field and buried them there; and there sprang up on the spot a birch tree -- a very lovely birch tree.

Some time had passed away -- who can tell how long they might have been living there? -- when the witch, to whom a child had been born in the meantime, began to take an ill-will to the man's daughter, and to torment her in all sorts of ways.

Now it happened that a great festival was to be held at the palace, and the king had commanded that all the people should be invited, and that this proclamation should be made:

"Come, people all!
Poor and wretched, one and all!
Blind and crippled though ye be,
Mount your steeds or come by sea."

And so they drove into the king's feast all the outcasts, and the maimed, and the halt, and the blind. In the good man's house, too, preparations were made to go to the palace. The witch said to the man, "Go you on in front, old man, with our youngest; I will give the elder girl work to keep her from being dull in our absence."

So the man took the child and set out. But the witch kindled a fire on the hearth, threw a potful of barleycorns among the cinders, and said to the girl, "If you have not picked the barley out of the ashes, and put it all back in the pot before nightfall, I shall eat you up!"

Then she hastened after the others, and the poor girl stayed at home and wept. She tried to be sure to pick up the grains of barley, but she soon saw how useless her labor was; and so she went in her sore trouble to the birch tree on her mother's grave, and cried and cried, because her mother lay dead beneath the sod and could help her no longer. In the midst of her grief she suddenly heard her mother's voice speak from the grave, and say to her, "Why do you weep, little daughter?"

"The witch has scattered barleycorns on the hearth, and bid me pick them out of the ashes," said the girl; "that is why I weep, dear little mother."

"Do not weep," said her mother consolingly. "Break off one of my branches, and strike the hearth with it crosswise, and all will be put right."

The girl did so. She struck the hearth with the birchen branch, and lo! the barleycorns flew into the pot, and the hearth was clean. Then she went back to the birch tree and laid the branch upon the grave. Then her mother bade her bathe on one side of the stem, dry herself on another, and dress on the third. When the girl had done all that, she had grown so lovely that no one on earth could rival her. Splendid clothing was given to her, and a horse, with hair partly of gold, partly of silver, and partly of something more precious still. The girl sprang into the saddle, and rode as swift as an arrow to the palace.

As she turned into the courtyard of the castle the king's son came out to meet her, tied her steed to a pillar, and led her in. He never left her side as they passed through the castle rooms; and all the people gazed at her, and wondered who the lovely maiden was, and from what castle she came; but no one knew her -- no one knew anything about her. At the banquet the prince invited her to sit next him in the place of honor; but the witch's daughter gnawed the bones under the table. The prince did not see her, and thinking it was a dog, he gave her such a push with his foot that her arm was broken. Are you not sorry for the witch's daughter? It was not her fault that her mother was a witch.

Towards evening the good man's daughter thought it was time to go home; but as she went, her ring caught on the latch of the door, for the king's son had had it smeared with tar. She did not take time to pull it off, but, hastily unfastening her horse from the pillar, she rode away beyond the castle walls as swift as an arrow. Arrived at home, she took off her clothes by the birch tree, left her horse standing there, and hastened to her place behind the stove. In a short time the man and the woman came home again too, and the witch said to the girl, "Ah! you poor thing, there you are to be sure! You don't know what fine times we have had at the palace! The king's son carried my daughter about, but the poor thing fell and broke her arm."

The girl knew well how matters really stood, but she pretended to know nothing about it, and sat dumb behind the stove.

The next day they were invited again to the king's banquet.

"Hey! old man," said the witch, "get on your clothes as quick as you can; we are bidden to the feast. Take you the child; I will give the other one work, lest she weary."

She kindled the fire, threw a potful of hemp seed among the ashes, and said to the girl, "If you do not get this sorted, and all the seed back into the pot, I shall kill you!"

The girl wept bitterly; then she went to the birch tree, washed herself on one side of it and dried herself on the other; and this time still finer clothes were given to her, and a very beautiful steed. She broke off a branch of the birch tree, struck the hearth with it, so that the seeds flew into the pot, and then hastened to the castle.

Again the king's son came out to meet her, tied her horse to a pillar, and led her into the banqueting hall. At the feast the girl sat next him in the place of honor, as she had done the day before. But the witch's daughter gnawed bones under the table, and the prince gave her a push by mistake, which broke her leg -- he had never noticed her crawling about among the people's feet. She was very unlucky!

The good man's daughter hastened home again betimes, but the king's son had smeared the door-posts with tar, and the girl's golden circlet stuck to it. She had not time to look for it, but sprang to the saddle and rode like an arrow to the birch tree. There she left her horse and her fine clothes, and said to her mother, "I have lost my circlet at the castle; the door-post was tarred, and it stuck fast."

"And even had you lost two of them," answered her mother, "I would give you finer ones."

Then the girl hastened home, and when her father came home from the feast with the witch, she was in her usual place behind the stove. Then the witch said to her, "You poor thing! what is there to see here compared with what we have seen at the palace? The king's son carried my daughter from one room to another; he let her fall, 'tis true, and my child's foot was broken."

The man's daughter held her peace all the time, and busied herself about the hearth.

The night passed, and when the day began to dawn, the witch awakened her husband, crying, "Hi! get up, old man! We are bidden to the royal banquet."

So the old man got up. Then the witch gave him the child, saying, "Take you the little one; I will give the other girl work to do, else she will weary at home alone."

She did as usual. This time it was a dish of milk she poured upon the ashes, saying, "If you do not get all the milk into the dish again before I come home, you will suffer for it."

How frightened the girl was this time! She ran to the birch tree, and by its magic power her task was accomplished; and then she rode away to the palace as before. When she got to the courtyard she found the prince waiting for her. He led her into the hall, where she was highly honored; but the witch's daughter sucked the bones under the table, and crouching at the people's feet she got an eye knocked out, poor thing! Now no one knew any more than before about the good man's daughter, no one knew whence she came; but the prince had had the threshold smeared with tar, and as she fled her gold slippers stuck to it. She reached the birch tree, and laying aside her finery, she said, "Alas I dear little mother, I have lost my gold slippers!"

"Let them be," was her mother's reply; "if you need them I shall give you finer ones."

Scarcely was she in her usual place behind the stove when her father came home with the witch. Immediately the witch began to mock her, saying, "Ah! you poor thing, there is nothing for you to see here, and we -- ah! what great things we have seen at the palace! My little girl was carried about again, but had the ill-luck to fall and get her eye knocked out. You stupid thing, you, what do you know about anything?"

"Yes, indeed, what can I know?" replied the girl; "I had enough to do to get the hearth clean."

Now the prince had kept all the things the girl had lost, and he soon set about finding the owner of them. For this purpose a great banquet was given on the fourth day, and all the people were invited to the palace. The witch got ready to go too. She tied a wooden beetle on where her child's foot should have been, a log of wood instead of an arm, and stuck a bit of dirt in the empty socket for an eye, and took the child with her to the castle. When all the people were gathered together, the king's son stepped in among the crowd and cried, "The maiden whose finger this ring slips over, whose head this golden hoop encircles, and whose foot this shoe fits, shall be my bride."

What a great trying on there was now among them all! The things would fit no one, however.

"The cinder wench is not here," said the prince at last; "go and fetch her, and let her try on the things."

So the girl was fetched, and the prince was just going to hand the ornaments to her, when the witch held him back, saying, "Don't give them to her; she soils everything with cinders; give them to my daughter rather."

Well, then the prince gave the witch's daughter the ring, and the woman filed and pared away at her daughter's finger till the ring fitted. It was the same with the circlet and the shoes of gold. The witch would not allow them to be handed to the cinder wench; she worked at her own daughter's head and feet till she got the things forced on. What was to be done now? The prince had to take the witch's daughter for his bride whether he would or no; he sneaked away to her father's house with her, however, for he was ashamed to hold the wedding festivities at the palace with so strange a bride. Some days passed, and at last he had to take his bride home to the palace, and he got ready to do so. Just as they were taking leave, the kitchen wench sprang down from her place by the stove, on the pretext of fetching something from the cowhouse, and in going by she whispered in the prince's ear as he stood in the yard, "Alas! dear prince, do not rob me of my silver and my gold."

Thereupon the king's son recognized the cinder wench; so he took both the girls with him, and set out. After they had gone some little way they came to the bank of a river, and the prince threw the witch's daughter across to serve as a bridge, and so got over with the cinder wench. There lay the witch's daughter then, like a bridge over the river, and could not stir, though her heart was consumed with grief. No help was near, so she cried at last in her anguish, "May there grow a golden hemlock out of my body! perhaps my mother will know me by that token."

Scarcely had she spoken when a golden hemlock sprang up from her, and stood upon the bridge.

Now, as soon as the prince had got rid of the witch's daughter he greeted the cinder wench as his bride, and they wandered together to the birch tree which grew upon the mother's grave. There they received all sorts of treasures and riches, three sacks full of gold, and as much silver, and a splendid steed, which bore them home to the palace. There they lived a long time together, and the young wife bore a son to the prince. Immediately word was brought to the witch that her daughter had borne a son -- for they all believed the young king's wife to be the witch's daughter.

"So, so," said the witch to herself; "I had better away with my gift for the infant, then."

And so saying she set out. Thus it happened that she came to the bank of the river, and there she saw the beautiful golden hemlock growing in the middle of the bridge, and when she began to cut it down to take to her grandchild, she heard a voice moaning, "Alas! dear mother, do not cut me so!"

"Are you here?" demanded the witch.

"Indeed I am, dear little mother," answered the daughter "They threw me across the river to make a bridge of me."

In a moment the witch had the bridge shivered to atoms, and then she hastened away to the palace. Stepping up to the young Queen's bed, she began to try her magic arts upon her, saying, "Spit, you wretch, on the blade of my knife; bewitch my knife's blade for me, and I shall change you into a reindeer of the forest."

"Are you there again to bring trouble upon me?" said the young woman.

She neither spat nor did anything else, but still the witch changed her into a reindeer, and smuggled her own daughter into her place as the prince's wife. But now the child grew restless and cried, because it missed its mother's care. They took it to the court, and tried to pacify it in every conceivable way, but its crying never ceased.

"What makes the child so restless?" asked the prince, and he went to a wise widow woman to ask her advice.

"Ay, ay, your own wife is not at home," said the widow woman; "she is living like a reindeer in the wood; you have the witch's daughter for a wife now, and the witch herself for a mother-in-law."

"Is there any way of getting my own wife back from the wood again?" asked the prince.

"Give me the child," answered the widow woman. "I'll take it with me tomorrow when I go to drive the cows to the wood. I'll make a rustling among the birch leaves and a trembling among the aspens -- perhaps the boy will grow quiet when he hears it."

"Yes, take the child away, take it to the wood with you to quiet it," said the prince, and led the widow woman into the castle.

"How now? you are going to send the child away to the wood?" said the witch in a suspicious tone, and tried to interfere.

But the king's son stood firm by what he had commanded, and said, "Carry the child about the wood; perhaps that will pacify it."

So the widow woman took the child to the wood. She came to the edge of a marsh, and seeing a herd of reindeer there, she began all at once to sing:

"Little Bright-eyes, little Redskin,
Come nurse the child you bore!
That bloodthirsty monster,
That man-eater grim,
Shall nurse him, shall tend him no more.
They may threaten and force as they will,
He turns from her, shrinks from her still,"

And immediately the reindeer drew near, and nursed and tended the child the whole day long; but at nightfall it had to follow the herd, and said to the widow woman, "Bring me the child tomorrow, and again the following day; after that I must wander with the herd far away to other lands."

The following morning the widow woman went back to the castle to fetch the child. The witch interfered, of course, but the prince said, "Take it, and carry it about in the open air; the boy is quieter at night, to be sure, when he has been in the wood all day."

So the widow took the child in her arms, and carried it to the marsh in the forest. There she sang as on the preceding day:

"Little Bright-eyes, little Redskin,
Come nurse the child you bore!
That bloodthirsty monster,
That man-eater grim,
Shall nurse him, shall tend him no more.
They may threaten and force as they will,
He turns from her, shrinks from her still,"

and immediately the reindeer left the herd and came to the child, and tended it as on the day before. And so it was that the child throve, till not a finer boy was to be seen anywhere. But the king's son had been pondering over all these things, and he said to the widow woman, "Is there no way of changing the reindeer into a human being again?"

"I don't rightly know," was her answer. "Come to the wood with me, however; when the woman puts off her reindeer skin I shall comb her head for her; whilst I am doing so you must burn the skin."

Thereupon they both went to the wood with the child; scarcely were they there when the reindeer appeared and nursed the child as before. Then the widow woman said to the reindeer, "Since you are going far away tomorrow, and I shall not see you again, let me comb your head for the last time, as a remembrance of you."

Good; the young woman stripped off the reindeer skin, and let the widow woman do as she wished. In the meantime the king's son threw the reindeer skin into the fire unobserved.

"What smells of singeing here?" asked the young woman, and looking round she saw her own husband. "Woe is me! you have burnt my skin. Why did you do that?"

"To give you back your human form again."

"Alack-a-day! I have nothing to cover me now, poor creature that I am!" cried the young woman, and transformed herself first into a distaff, then into a wooden beetle, then into a spindle, and into all imaginable shapes. But all these shapes the king's son went on destroying till she stood before him in human form again.

"Alas! wherefore take me home with you again," cried the young woman, "since the witch is sure to eat me up?"

"She will not eat you up," answered her husband; and they started for home with the child.

But when the witch wife saw them she ran away with her daughter, and if she has not stopped she is running still, though at a great age. And the prince, and his wife, and the baby lived happy ever afterwards.

Maria and the Golden Slipper by Dean Fansler

ONCE there lived a couple who had an only daughter, Maria. When Maria was a little girl, her mother died. A few years later Maria's father fell in love with a widow named Juana, who had two daughters. The elder of these daughters was Rosa, and the younger was Damiana. When Maria was grown to be a young woman, her father married the woman Juana. Maria continued to live with her father and stepmother. But Juana and her two daughters treated Maria as a servant. She had to do all the work in the house: cook the food, wash the clothes, clean the floors. The only clothes she herself had to wear were ragged and dirty.

One day Prince Malecadel wanted to get married, so he gave a ball, to which he invited all the ladies in his kingdom. He said that the most beautiful of all was to be his wife.

When Damiana and Rosa knew that all the ladies were invited, they began to discuss what clothes they would wear to the ball; but poor Maria was in the river, washing the clothes. Maria was very sad and was weeping, for she had no clothes at all in which she could appear at the prince's fête.

While she was washing, a crab approached her, and said, "Why are you crying, Maria? Tell me the reason, for I am your mother."

Then Maria said to the crab, "I am treated by my aunt and sisters as a servant; and there will be a ball tonight, but I have no clothes to wear."

While she was talking to the crab, Juana came up. The stepmother was very angry with Maria, and ordered her to catch the crab and cook it for their dinner. Maria seized the crab and carried it to the house. At first she did not want to cook it, for she knew that it was her mother; but Juana whipped her so hard, that at last she was forced to obey.

Before it was put in the earthen pot to be cooked, the crab said to Maria, "Maria, don't eat my flesh, but collect all my shell after I am eaten, and bury the pieces in the garden near the house. They will grow into a tree, and you can have what you want if you will only ask the tree for it."

After her parents had eaten the flesh of the crab, Maria collected all its shell and buried it in the garden. At twilight she saw a tree standing on the very spot where she had buried the shell.

When night came, Rosa and Damiana went to the ball, and Juana retired for the night as soon as her daughters were gone. When Maria saw that her aunt was sleeping, she went into the garden and asked the tree for what she wanted. The tree changed her clothes into very beautiful ones, and furnished her with a fine coach drawn by four fine horses, and a pair of golden slippers.

Before she left, the tree said to her, "You must be in your house before twelve o'clock. If you are not, your clothes will be changed into ragged, dirty ones again, and your coach will disappear."

After promising to remember the warning of the tree, Maria went to the ball, where she was received by the prince very graciously. All the ladies were astonished when they saw her; she was the most beautiful of all. Then she sat between her two sisters, but neither Rosa nor Damiana recognized her. The prince danced with her all the time. When Maria saw that it was half-past eleven, she bade farewell to the prince and all the ladies present, and went home. When she reached the garden, the tree changed her beautiful clothes back into her old ones, and the coach disappeared. Then she went to bed and to sleep. When her sisters came home, they told her of everything that had happened at the ball.

The next night the prince gave another ball. After Rosa and Damiana had dressed themselves in their best clothes and gone, Maria again went to the garden to ask for beautiful clothes. This time she was given a coach drawn by five (?) horses, and again the tree warned her to return before twelve. The prince was delighted to see her, and danced with her the whole evening. Maria was so enchanted that she forgot to notice the time. While she was dancing, she heard the clock striking twelve. She ran as fast as she could down stairs and out the palace door, but in her haste she dropped one of her golden slippers. This night she had to walk home, and in her old ragged clothes, too. One of her golden slippers she had with her; but the other, which she had dropped at the door, was found by one of the guards, who gave it to the prince. The guard said that the slipper had been lost by the beautiful lady who ran out of the palace when the clock was striking twelve.

Then the prince said to all the people present, "The lady whom this slipper fits is to be my wife."

The next morning the prince ordered one of his guards to carry the slipper to every house in the city to see if its owner could be found. The first house visited was the one in which Maria lived. Rosa tried to put the slipper on her foot, but her foot was much too big. Then Damiana put it on her foot, but her foot was too small. The two sisters tried and tried again to make the slipper fit, but in vain.

Then Maria told them that she would try, and see if the slipper would fit her foot; but her sisters said to her, "Your feet are very dirty. This golden slipper will not go on your foot, for your feet are larger than ours." And they laughed at her.

But the guard who had brought the slipper said, "Let her try. It is the prince's order that all shall try."

So he gave it to Maria. Then Maria put it on, and it fitted her foot exactly. She then drew the other slipper from underneath her dress, and put it on her other foot. When the two sisters saw the two slippers on Maria's feet, they almost fainted with astonishment.

So Maria became the wife of the prince, and from that time on she was very dear to her sisters and aunt.

The Turkey Herd by Elsie Clews Parsons

Long ago at Kyakima lived a girl who spent all her time herding turkeys. She never did anything for her sisters. Nobody would comb her hair. It was all in a snarl. Her sisters would tell her to cook. They would say, "Why do you so love the turkeys?" She did not answer. After her sisters had cooked, she would take the bread and go out and tend the turkeys.

At Matsaki they were dancing lapalehakya.

They were dancing for the third time, when the turkey girl said, "Younger sisters!"

The turkeys said, "What?"

The girl said, "I want to go and see the dance."

The turkeys said, "You are too dirty to go."

She repeated, "I want to go." The turkeys said, "Let us eat the lice out of her hair!"

Then each ate lice from her hair.

Then an elder-sister (kyauu) turkey clapped her wings, and down from the air fell women's moccasins (mokwawe). Then her younger sister (ikina) clapped her wings, and down from the air fell a blanket dress (yatone). Then another elder sister clapped her wings, and down from the air fell a belt (ehnina). A younger sister clapped her wings, and a pitone fell down. An elder sister clapped, and a blanket (eha) fell down. The little younger sister (an hani tsanna) clapped, and a hair belt (tsutokehnina) fell down.

An kyauu said, "Is this all you want?"

The girl said, "Yes." She put on the moccasins and the ehayatonana.

The turkeys put up her hair in a queue.

She said to the turkeys, "I will come back before sundown."

She went to her house, and made a little cloth bag, and filled it with meal. Then she went on to Matsaki.

Her sisters said, "Has she gone to the dance?"

One said, "Yes."

"She is too dirty to go."

After she reached Matsaki, as she stood there, the dance director (otakya mosi) asked if she would dance.

She said, "Yes." She danced all day. When the sun set, she finished dancing, and ran back to the turkeys.

The turkeys had said, when she did not come, "We must not go on living here. Our sister does not love us."

When she arrived, they were not there. They were on top of a little hill, singing:

Kyana to to
kyana to to
kyana to to ye
uli uli uli to to to to

They flew down to Kyakima. They went on as fast as they could until they came to turkey tracks (tonateanawa). There they drank at the spring. Their tracks were from north, south, east, west. After they drank, they flew to Shoakoskwikwi. They reached a high rock. They sat on it, and sang:

Kyana to to
kyana to to
kyana to to ye
uli uli uli to to to to.

When awan kyauu arrived, the turkeys were not there. She saw their tracks. She followed the tracks on a run. At Tonateanawa she saw where they had drunk. She ran on. Then she lost their tracks. She went back to her house. The turkeys had flown to Shoakoskwikwi, to the spring there. That is why at Shoakoskwikwi you see wild turkeys. The girl came back to her house crying.

Her sisters said, "Don't cry! You did not return on time. You did not love them."

The girl stayed and cooked for her sisters. Thus it was long ago.

The Indian Cinderella by Cyrus Macmillan

On the shores of a wide bay on the Atlantic coast there dwelt in old times a great Indian warrior. It was said that he had been one of Glooskap's best helpers and friends, and that he had done for him many wonderful deeds. But that, no man knows. He had, however, a very wonderful and strange power; he could make himself invisible; he could thus mingle unseen with his enemies and listen to their plots. He was known among the people as Strong Wind, the Invisible. He dwelt with his sister in a tent near the sea, and his sister helped him greatly in his work. Many maidens would have been glad to marry him, and he was much sought after because of his mighty deeds; and it was known that Strong Wind would marry the first maiden who could see him as he came home at night. Many made the trial, but it was a long time before one succeeded.

Strong Wind used a clever trick to test the truthfulness of all who sought to win him. Each evening as the day went down, his sister walked on the beach with any girl who wished to make the trial. His sister could always see him, but no one else could see him. And as he came home from work in the twilight, his sister as she saw him drawing near would ask the girl who sought him, "Do you see him?"

And each girl would falsely answer "Yes."

And his sister would ask, "With what does he draw his sled?"

And each girl would answer, "With the hide of a moose," or "With a pole," or "With a great cord."

And then his sister would know that they all had lied, for their answers were mere guesses. And many tried and lied and failed, for Strong Wind would not marry any who were untruthful.

There lived in the village a great chief who had three daughters. Their mother had long been dead. One of these was much younger than the others. She was very beautiful and gentle and well beloved by all, and for that reason her older sisters were very jealous of her charms and treated her very cruelly. They clothed her in rags that she might be ugly; and they cut off her long black hair; and they burned her face with coals from the fire that she might be scarred and disfigured. And they lied to their father, telling him that she had done these things herself. But the young girl was patient and kept her gentle heart and went gladly about her work.

Like other girls, the chief's two eldest daughters tried to win Strong Wind. One evening, as the day went down, they walked on the shore with Strong Wind's sister and waited for his coming. Soon he came home from his day's work, drawing his sled. And his sister asked as usual, "Do you see him?"

And each one, lying, answered "Yes."

And she asked, "Of what is his shoulder strap made?"

And each, guessing, said "Of rawhide."

Then they entered the tent where they hoped to see Strong Wind eating his supper; and when he took off his coat and his moccasins they could see them, but more than these they saw nothing. And Strong Wind knew that they had lied, and he kept himself from their sight, and they went home dismayed.

One day the chief's youngest daughter with her rags and her burnt face resolved to seek Strong Wind. She patched her clothes with bits of birch bark from the trees, and put on the few little ornaments she possessed, and went forth to try to see the Invisible One as all the other girls of the village had done before. And her sisters laughed at her and called her "fool"; and as she passed along the road all the people laughed at her because of her tattered frock and her burnt face, but silently she went her way.

Strong Wind's sister received the little girl kindly, and at twilight she took her to the beach. Soon Strong Wind came home drawing his sled. And his sister asked, "Do you see him?"

And the girl answered "No," and his sister wondered greatly because she spoke the truth.

And again she asked, "Do you see him now?"

And the girl answered, "Yes, and he is very wonderful."

And she asked, "With what does he draw his sled?"

And the girl answered, "With the Rainbow," and she was much afraid.

And she asked further, "Of what is his bowstring?"

And the girl answered, "His bowstring is the Milky Way."

Then Strong Wind's sister knew that because the girl had spoken the truth at first her brother had made himself visible to her. And she said, "Truly, you have seen him." And she took her home and bathed her, and all the scars disappeared from her face and body; and her hair grew long and black again like the raven's wing; and she gave her fine clothes to wear and many rich ornaments. Then she bade her take the wife's seat in the tent.

Soon Strong Wind entered and sat beside her, and called her his bride. The very next day she became his wife, and ever afterwards she helped him to do great deeds.

The girl's two elder sisters were very cross and they wondered greatly at what had taken place. But Strong Wind, who knew of their cruelty, resolved to punish them. Using his great power, he changed them both into aspen trees and rooted them in the earth. And since that day the leaves of the aspen have always trembled, and they shiver in fear at the approach of Strong Wind, it matters not how softly he comes, for they are still mindful of his great power and anger because of their lies and their cruelty to their sister long ago.

The Little Gold Shoe by Jeremy Thorpe

THERE was once a King in the Western Highlands whose Queen died, leaving with him a baby daughter.

The Queen had been good and kind and beautiful and the King grieved long and sorely for her; and, indeed, all his subjects in the west country shared his sorrow. But as time went on everyone was agreed that it would be much better for the King as well as for the little Princess that he should take to himself a new Queen. And in due time the King saw that for himself, and he married again.

The new Queen was quite kind to the daughter of the first Queen, even when she had a little daughter of her own. But when the two Princesses were growing up and the Queen saw how much more beautiful the elder girl was than her own daughter, her feelings began to change. And jealousy -- the monster with the green eye -- came and dwelt in her breast, and caused her to be very cruel to her stepdaughter. She used to beat her very often, and she gave her very little to eat -- and by and by she sent her out into the far-away field to herd the sheep. The poor young Princess had no one to help her. She could not appeal to the King, because he was away making war on another King in the Western Isles -- and in his absence the Queen had complete authority over his kingdom.

The poor girl used to sit in the far-away field among the sheep, weeping quietly, and thinking how much better off they were than herself. But one member of the flock was sad when he saw her grief, for he loved his gentle shepherdess.

This was an old grey-horned sheep, but for whom she would certainly have starved, for he used to bring her food every day. And it greatly puzzled the cruel Queen to see that, although she gave her stepdaughter no food, she was not wasting away. So the Queen asked the henwife of the Palace -- and a wicked creature she was! -- to try and find out whether someone was bringing food to the Princess; and the henwife sent her daughter into the far-away field to spy on her. This girl, who was very sly and ugly, had -- over and above the usual two eyes of other people --a n invisible eye in the back of her head.

All day long she stayed out in the far-away field watching the Princess, who was growing hungrier and hungrier! But she dared not ask the grey-horned sheep for food, in case the henwife's daughter should see.

At last the latter began to yawn widely, and the Princess said to her: "Oh, poor girl, how tired you are! Do lie down and put your head on my knee and I will stroke your hair. And you will have a lovely sleep!"

The henwife's daughter, who was not a bit sleepy but only very bored, said she would do as the Princess proposed. And she laid her head on the Princess's knee and let her stroke her ugly hair. And presently her eyes closed and she pretended to be sleeping.

But her invisible eye was watching, and it saw the Princess beckon gently to the grey-horned sheep; and when the sheep came trotting up with food for her the eye saw that also. So the henwife's daughter went home and told it to the henwife, who told it to the Queen, that the grey-horned sheep was giving food to the Princess.

The Queen was very angry, and she sent the henwife for the Palace butcher, and gave him this order: "Go at once and kill the grey-horned sheep that is in the far-away field. Bring his flesh to be used in the Palace, but leave his skin and his bones in the field as a warning to the rest of the flock."

When the Princess saw the butcher coming she was very much distressed for her friend's sake, but the grey-horned sheep said: "You need not weep because I am going to be killed. Only wait until the butcher has gone away, then gather up my bones and roll them in my skin. You will see that I will come alive again and continue to help you."

And the Princess did what he told her, except that she forgot to put the sheep's trotters into his skin, so when he came alive again he was lame! But in spite of that he hobbled to meet her every day with food. And the Princess grew prettier and prettier, and the Queen grew more and more jealous for her own daughter.

One day a handsome young Prince from the southwest of Scotland came to hunt in the Western Highlands, and he saw a beautiful young girl herding sheep in a field. He stopped, enchanted, and he said to the nobles who were with him: "Find out who that beautiful girl is. I have never seen anyone so lovely!"

When the nobles asked the country people about her they were told that the lovely shepherdess was a Princess whose stepmother was very unkind to her; and that while everyone was sorry for her, no one had the right to interfere with her stepmother's treatment of her.

By this time the young Prince had fallen deeply in love with the Princess, and he came again and again to the far-away field where she was herding, in order to look at her and talk to her. He told his nobles that -- stepmother or no stepmother -- he had made up his mind to marry her!

When it came to the knowledge of the henwife that a rich and handsome Prince was courting the Princess, she ran and told the Queen, who, furious at the idea of her stepdaughter making a good match, declared that the affair must be stopped forthwith. So the Princess was ordered to leave the far-away field, and the Queen sent her own daughter there in place of her. She hoped that the Prince might prefer her to her stepsister -- which, of course, was absurd!

She sent her stepdaughter to work as a servant in the Palace kitchen, and she gave her clothes of the servants to wear. The Princess missed the fresh air of the fields very badly, and perhaps she missed the Prince also ! Anyhow, she took every chance of stealing out for a little while into the fresh evening air, and she generally found the Prince waiting on the chance of seeing her.

One day he brought her a present -- a pair of beautiful golden shoes, which fitted her dainty feet to perfection. She was so pleased with them -- and with their giver -- that she stayed longer than usual with him; and when she realized how time had passed she took fright and started to run back to the Palace as quickly as possible. In her haste she dropped one of her golden shoes, and she was afraid to wait to pick it up. So the Prince picked up the little golden shoe and he ran after her; but when he reached the Palace the great gate was closed. On the following day he took the golden shoe with him and went boldly to the Palace. He was just about to knock on the gate when it opened to let the Queen come out.

"Well?" she said graciously to the handsome young man. "Well, who are you, and what do you want?"

Showing her the little olden shoe in his hand he said to her: "Do you see this shoe? Its fellow is already within your gates, and I will marry the one whose foot it fits."

The Queen did a bit of quick thinking, and then -- taking the shoe from his hand -- he said to the Prince: "Come along into the Palace then, and I shall help you to find the one whose foot this shoe will fit."

She led him indoors, and after inviting him to wait in one of the reception rooms she ran to the kitchen. There her stepdaughter was cooking the dinner, and the Queen hustled her into a curious sort of niche at the back of the fire-place and told her that on no account was she to come out until she was given permission to do so.

Then she sent for her own daughter, and when she came the Queen told her to try on the little golden shoe.

"Oh mother!" the girl said, "I could never wear this shoe. It is far too small! No one except my sister has such tiny feet!"

"Stuff and nonsense!" the Queen said angrily. "Are you going to allow a little discomfort to stand in your own light ? You must put on this shoe!"

And she called the henwife to come in, saying to her: "My daughter is to get that shoe on as quickly as possible. If the shoe will not fit the foot, make the foot fit the shoe!"

So the henwife seized the younger Princess's foot, and, regardless of her cries, she cut off the points of her toes and succeeded in thrusting her foot into the golden shoe.

"There you are!" she said. "It is a perfect fit!"

And the Queen went and fetched the Prince, saying to him: "Here is your bride! See how perfectly the shoe fits her!"

The poor Prince was naturally much taken aback at this turn of affairs! He had not imagined that there could be another foot in the whole world small enough to wear the little golden shoe! He did not know what to do, for he had definitely told the Queen that he would marry the one whose foot the shoe would fit---and there was no sign anywhere of his shepherdess.

The Queen insisted on sending out invitations to the Prince's wedding with her daughter, which she decided was to take place on the following day. The Prince could not sleep all night for perplexity, and when morning came the wedding guests began to arrive, and there seemed to be no escape for him! Soon a large and brilliant company was assembled; and the priest was just about to begin the marriage service when a bird came and alighted on the window sill, and said: "The blood's in the shoe, and the pretty foot's in the niche at the back of the fire!"

"What is that bird saying?" the young bridegroom asked.

"Never mind the bird -- a horrid, beaky, lying creature!" replied the Queen. "Let the wedding go on!"

But, though she tried to chase it away, the bird returned again and yet again to the window sill; and the third time the Prince said: "I must hear what this bird is trying to tell us." And he went to the window, where he heard the bird say plainly, " The blood's in the shoe, and the pretty foot's in the niche at the back of the fire."

Then he turned to the Queen and said: "I am going to find out what he means by the niche at the back of the fire." And he left the room, to the chagrin of the Queen and the amazement of all the guests.

Room after room of the Palace he searched without success, but when he came to the kitchen he found the niche at the back of the fire, and standing in it, with a little golden shoe on one foot, was his beautiful shepherdess!

The Queen stamped and raged at the failure of her scheming, and she was still more angry when her own daughter -- who had suffered agony when her toes were cut -- kicked off the golden shoe that she wore, and said: "There you are! Take it away! I cannot bear it any longer."

And indeed it was little wonder that she wanted to get rid of the shoe, for it was full of blood!

The Prince's servants took and cleaned all the blood off it, and it slipped sweetly over the elder Princess's foot alongside of its fellow.

Never had such beautiful little feet been seen, and the Prince knelt down and kissed first one little golden shoe and then the other. Then, rising, he took the Princess by the hand and said:

"Thanks to the bird, I have found in the niche at the back of the fire my beautiful Princess with the dainty feet; there is now no blood in the shoes of gold!"

He took her away to his kingdom in the south-west, and there they were married and lived happily ever after. And the Princess always wore golden shoes.

The Twelve Months by Alexander Chodzko

THERE was once a widow who had two daughters, Helen, her own child by her dead husband, and Marouckla, his daughter by his first wife. She loved Helen, but hated the poor orphan because she was far prettier than her own daughter.

Marouckla did not think about her good looks, and could not understand why her stepmother should be angry at the sight of her. The hardest work fell to her share. She cleaned out the rooms, cooked, washed, sewed, spun, wove, brought in the hay, milked the cow, and all this without any help.

Helen, meanwhile, did nothing but dress herself in her best clothes and go to one amusement after another.

But Marouckla never complained. She bore the scoldings and bad temper of mother and sister with a smile on her lips, and the patience of a lamb. But this angelic behavior did not soften them. They became even more tyrannical and grumpy, for Marouckla grew daily more beautiful, while Helen's ugliness increased. So the stepmother determined to get rid of Marouckla, for she knew that while she remained, her own daughter would have no suitors. Hunger, every kind of privation, abuse, every means was used to make the girl's life miserable. But in spite of it all Marouckla grew ever sweeter and more charming.

One day in the middle of winter Helen wanted some wood-violets.

"Listen," cried she to Marouckla, "you must go up the mountain and find me violets. I want some to put in my gown. They must be fresh and sweet-scented-do you hear?"

"But, my dear sister, whoever heard of violets blooming in the snow?" said the poor orphan.

"You wretched creature! Do you dare to disobey me?" said Helen. "Not another word. Off with you! If you do not bring me some violets from the mountain forest I will kill you."

The stepmother also added her threats to those of Helen, and with vigorous blows they pushed Marouckla outside and shut the door upon her. The weeping girl made her way to the mountain. The snow lay deep, and there was no trace of any human being. Long she wandered hither and thither, and lost herself in the wood. She was hungry, and shivered with cold, and prayed to die.

Suddenly she saw a light in the distance, and climbed toward it till she reached the top of the mountain. Upon the highest peak burned a large fire, surrounded by twelve blocks of stone on which sat twelve strange beings. Of these the first three had white hair, three were not quite so old, three were young and handsome, and the rest still younger.

There they all sat silently looking at the fire. They were the Twelve Months of the Year. The great January was placed higher than the others. His hair and mustache were white as snow, and in his hand he held a wand. At first Marouckla was afraid, but after a while her courage returned, and drawing near, she said: --

"Men of God, may I warm myself at your fire? I am chilled by the winter cold."

The great January raised his head and answered: "What brings thee here, my daughter? What dost thou seek?"

"I am looking for violets," replied the maiden.

"This is not the season for violets. Dost thou not see the snow everywhere?" said January.

"I know well, but my sister Helen and my stepmother have ordered me to bring them violets from your mountain. If I return without them they will kill me. I pray you, good shepherds, tell me where they may be found."

Here the great January arose and went over to the youngest of the Months, and, placing his wand in his hand, said: -- "Brother March, do thou take the highest place."

March obeyed, at the same time waving his wand over the fire. Immediately the flames rose toward the sky, the snow began to melt and the trees and shrubs to bud. The grass became green, and from between its blades peeped the pale primrose. It was spring, and the meadows were blue with violets.

"Gather them quickly, Marouckla," said March.

Joyfully she hastened to pick the flowers, and having soon a large bunch she thanked them and ran home. Helen and the stepmother were amazed at the sight of the flowers, the scent of which filled the house.

"Where did you find them?" asked Helen.

"Under the trees on the mountain-side," said Marouckla.

Helen kept the flowers for herself and her mother. She did not even thank her stepsister for the trouble she had taken. The next day she desired Marouckla to fetch her strawberries.

"Run," said she, "and fetch me strawberries from the mountain. They must be very sweet and ripe."

"But whoever heard of strawberries ripening in the snow?" exclaimed Marouckla.

"Hold your tongue, worm; don't answer me. If I don't have my strawberries I will kill you," said Helen.

Then the stepmother pushed Marouckla into the yard and bolted the door. The unhappy girl made her way toward the mountain and to the large fire round which sat the Twelve Months. The great January occupied the highest place.

"Men of God, may I warm myself at your fire? The winter cold chills me," said she, drawing near.

The great January raised his head and asked: "Why comest thou here? What dost thou seek?"

"I am looking for strawberries," said she.

"We are in the midst of winter," replied January, "strawberries do not grow in the snow."

"I know," said the girl sadly, "but my sister and stepmother have ordered me to bring them strawberries. If I do not they will kill me. Pray, good shepherds, tell me where to find them."

The great January arose, crossed over to the month opposite him, and putting the wand in his hand, said: "Brother June, do thou take the highest place." June obeyed, and as he waved his wand over the fire the flames leaped toward the sky. Instantly the snow melted, the earth was covered with verdure, trees were clothed with leaves, birds began to sing, and various flowers blossomed in the forest. It was summer. Under the bushes masses of star-shaped flowers changed into ripening strawberries, and instantly they covered the glade, making it look like a sea of blood.

"Gather them quickly, Marouckla," said June.

Joyfully she thanked the Months, and having filled her apron ran happily home.

Helen and her mother wondered at seeing the strawberries, which filled the house with their delicious fragrance.

"Wherever did you find them?" asked Helen crossly.

"Right up among the mountains. Those from under the beech trees are not bad," answered Marouckla.

Helen gave a few to her mother and ate the rest herself. Not one did she offer to her stepsister. Being tired of strawberries, on the third day she took a fancy for some fresh, red apples.

"Run, Marouckla," said she, "and fetch me fresh, red apples from the mountain."

"Apples in winter, sister? Why, the trees have neither leaves nor fruit!"

"Idle thing, go this minute," said Helen; "unless you bring back apples we will kill you."

As before, the stepmother seized her roughly and turned her out of the house. The poor girl went weeping up the mountain, across the deep snow, and on toward the fire round which were the Twelve Months. Motionless they sat there, and on the highest stone was the great January.

"Men of God, may I warm myself at your fire? The winter cold chills me," said she, drawing near.

The great January raised his head. "Why comest thou here? What does thou seek?" asked he.

"I am come to look for red apples," replied Marouckla.

"But this is winter, and not the season for red apples," observed the great January.

"I know," answered the girl, "but my sister and stepmother sent me to fetch red apples from the mountain. If I return without them they will kill me."

Thereupon the great January arose and went over to one of the elderly Months, to whom he handed the wand saying: --

"Brother September, do thou take the highest place."

September moved to the highest stone, and waved his wand over the fire. There was a flare of red flames, the snow disappeared, but the fading leaves which trembled on the trees were sent by a cold northeast wind in yellow masses to the glade. Only a few flowers of autumn were visible. At first Marouckla looked in vain for red apples. Then she espied a tree which grew at a great height, and from the branches of this hung the bright, red fruit. September ordered her to gather some quickly. The girl was delighted and shook the tree. First one apple fell, then another.

"That is enough," said September; "hurry home."

Thanking the Months she returned joyfully. Helen and the stepmother wondered at seeing the fruit.

"Where did you gather them?" asked the stepsister.

"There are more on the mountain-top," answered Marouckla.

"Then, why did you not bring more?" said Helen angrily. "You must have eaten them on your way back, you wicked girl."

"No, dear sister, I have not even tasted them," said Marouckla. "I shook the tree twice. One apple fell each time. Some shepherds would not allow me to shake it again, but told me to return home."

"Listen, mother," said Helen. "Give me my cloak. I will fetch some more apples myself. I shall be able to find the mountain and the tree. The shepherds may cry `Stop!' but I will not leave go till I have shaken down all the apples."

In spite of her mother's advice she wrapped herself in her pelisse, put on a warm hood, and took the road to the mountain. Snow covered everything. Helen lost herself and wandered hither and thither. After a while she saw a light above her, and, following in its direction, reached the mountain-top.

There was the flaming fire, the twelve blocks of stone, and the Twelve Months. At first she was frightened and hesitated; then she came nearer and warmed her hands. She did not ask permission, nor did she speak one polite word.

"What hath brought thee here? What dost thou seek?" said the great January severely.

"I am not obliged to tell you, old graybeard. What business is it of yours?" she replied disdainfully, turning her back on the fire and going toward the forest.

The great January frowned, and waved his wand over his head. Instantly the sky became covered with clouds, the fire went down, snow fell in large flakes, an icy wind howled round the mountain. Amid the fury of the storm Helen stumbled about. The pelisse failed to warm her benumbed limbs.

The mother kept on waiting for her. She looked from the window, she watched from the doorstep, but her daughter came not. The hours passed slowly, but Helen did not return.

"Can it be that the apples have charmed her from her home?" thought the mother. Then she clad herself in hood and pelisse, and went in search of her daughter. Snow fell in huge masses. It covered all things. For long she wandered hither and thither, the icy northeast wind whistled in the mountain, but no voice answered her cries.

Day after day Marouckla worked, and prayed, and waited, but neither stepmother nor sister returned. They had been frozen to death on the mountain.

The inheritance of a small house, a field, and a cow fell to Marouckla. In course of time an honest farmer came to share them with her, and their lives were happy and peaceful.

Yeh-Shen by Unknown

China (9th Century)

DURING the time of the Ch'in and IIan dynasties, a cave chief named Wu married two wives and each gave birth to baby girls. Before long Chief Wu and one wife died leaving one baby, Yeh-Shen, to be reared by her stepmother. The stepmother didn't like Yeh-Shen for she was more beautiful and kinder than her own daughter so she treated her poorly. Yeh-Shen was given the worse jobs and the only friend she had was a beautiful fish with big golden eyes.

Each day the fish came out of the water onto the bank to be fed by Yeh-Shen. Now Yen-Shen had little food for herself but she was willing to share with the fish. Her stepmother hearing about the fish disguised herself as Yen-Shen and enticed the fish from the water. She stabbed it with a dagger, and cooked the fish for dinner. Yeh-Shen was distraught when she learned of the fish's death. As she sat crying she heard a voice and looked up to see a wise old man wearing the coarsest of clothes and with hair hanging down over his shoulders.

He told her that the bones of the fish were filled with a powerful spirit, and that when she was in serious need she was to kneel before the bones and tell them of her heart's desires. She was warned not to waste their gifts. Yeh-Shen retrieved the bones from the trash heap and hid them in a safe place. Time passed and the spring festival was nearing. This was a time when the young people gathered in the village to meet one another and to find husbands and wives.

Yen-Shen longed to go to the festival but her stepmother wouldn't allow it because she feared that someone would pick Yeh-Shen rather than her own daughter. The stepmother and the daughter left for the festival leaving Yeh-Shen behind. Yeh-Shen wanting desperately to go asked the bones for clothes to wear to the festival. Suddenly she was wearing a beautiful gown of azure blue with a cloak of kingfisher feathers draped around her shoulders. On her feet were beautiful slippers.

They were woven of golden threads in a pattern of a scaled fish and the soles were made of solid gold. When she walked she felt lighter than air. She was warned not to lose the slippers. Yeh-Shen arrived at the festival and soon all were looking her way. The daughter and step-mother moved closer to her for they seemed to recognize this beautiful person.

Seeing that she would be found out, Yeh-Shen dashed out of the village leaving behind one of the golden slippers. When she arrived home she was dressed again in her rags. She spoke again to the bones, but they were now silent. Saddened she put the one golden slipper in her bedstraw. After a time a merchant found the lost slipper, and seeing the value in the golden slipper sold it to a merchant who gave it to the king of the island kingdom of T'o Han. Now the king wanted to find the owner of this tiny beautiful slipper. He sent his people to search the kingdom but no one's foot would fit in the tiny golden slipper. He had the slipper placed on display in a pavilion on the side of the road where the slipper had been found with an announcement that the shoe was to be returned to the owner.

The king's men waited out of site. All the women came to try on the shoe. One dark night Yeh-Shen slipped quietly across the pavilion, took the tiny golden slipper and turned to leave, but the king's men rushed out and arrested her. She was taken to the king who was furious for he couldn't believe that any one in rags could possibly own a golden slipper.

As he looked closer at her face he was struck by her beauty and he noticed she had the tiniest feet. The king and his men returned home with her where she produced the other slipper. As she slipped on the two slippers her rags turned into the beautiful gown and cloak she had worn to the festival. The king realized that she was the one for him. They married and lived happily ever after. However, the stepmother and daughter were never allowed to visit Yeh-Shen and were forced to continue to live in their cave until the day they were crushed to death in a shower of flying stones.

The Green Knight by Svendt Grundtvig

ONCE upon a time there were a king and a queen and they had but one little daughter, and when she was very young her dear mother became sick unto death. When the queen knew that she had only a short time to live, she called the king and said, "My dear lord and husband! in order that I may die in peace you must promise me one thing, and that is, that you will never refuse our child anything that she may ask of you if it be possible to grant her wish." That the king promised her and she died soon afterward.

The king's heart was nearly broken for he loved his wife devotedly, and his little daughter alone could comfort him. The princess grew up, and the fulfillment of the promise was indeed easy for the king; he never refused her a request. That spoiled her a little, but otherwise she was a dear, good child who only needed a mother to understand and love her; for the lack of this she was often moody and melancholy. The princess did not care for games and amusements like other children, but instead she liked to wander alone in the gardens and woods, and above all she loved flowers and birds and animals, and she was also fond of reading poetry and stories.

Not far from the palace there lived the widow of a count, who had a daughter a little older than the princess. The young countess, however, was not a good girl, but was vain, selfish and hard-hearted; on the other hand she was clever, like her mother, and could dissimulate when she thought it would serve her ends. The countess cleverly devised ways so that her daughter was often thrown together with the princess, and both mother and daughter spared no pains to please her. They did everything in their power to give her pleasure and cheer her, and soon she always had to have either one or the other by her side.

Now that was just what the countess wanted and had been working for; so that when she saw that she had brought matters to that point, she made her daughter tell the princess, amid tears, that they must now separate because she and her mother had to go far away into another country. Then the little princess ran at once to the countess and told her that she must not leave with her daughter, for she could not live without her and would grieve to death if she left her. Then the countess pretended to be deeply moved and told the princess that there was only one way that she could be persuaded to stay in the country, and that was for the king to marry her. Then both mother and daughter could always stay with her, and they painted in glowing colors the joys that would be hers if that should come to pass.

Then the princess went to her father, the king, and begged and implored him to marry the countess, for otherwise she would go away and his poor little daughter would lose her only friend and grieve to death.

"You would certainly repent of it, if I were to do it," said the king, "and I should also, for I have no desire whatever to marry, and I have no confidence in the deceitful countess and her deceitful daughter."

But the princess did not cease crying and imploring him until he promised to grant her wish. Then the king asked the countess to marry him and she at once consented. Soon after that the wedding ceremony took place and the countess became queen and was now the stepmother of the young princess.

But after the marriage all was changed. The queen did nothing but tease and torment her stepdaughter, while nothing was too good for her own child. Her daughter did not pay any attention to the poor princess, but did everything she could to make her life miserable.

The king, who could see all this, took it very much to heart, for he loved his daughter deeply; so he said to her on one occasion, "Alas, my poor little daughter, you are having a sad life and must certainly have repented many a time of that which you asked of me, for it has all turned out as I foretold. But now, unfortunately, it is too late. I think it would be better for you to leave us for a time and go out to my summer palace on the island; there you would, at least, have peace and quiet."

The princess agreed with her father, and although it was very hard for them to be separated, it was nevertheless absolutely necessary, as she could no longer endure her wicked stepmother and her malicious stepsister. So she took with her two of her ladies in waiting to live in the summer palace on the island, and her father came from time to time to visit her; and he could see very plainly that she was much happier here than she would have been at home with her wicked stepmother.

So she grew up to be a lovely maiden, pure, innocent and thoughtful, kind to both men and beasts. But she was never really happy, and there was always an undercurrent of sadness in her nature, and a longing for something better than she had hitherto found in the world.

One day her father came to her to bid her farewell, for he had to go on a long journey to be present at a gathering of kings and nobles from many lands, and would not return for a long time. The king wanted to cheer his daughter, so he said to her jestingly that he would look carefully among the princes to see whether he could not find one among them all who would be worthy to become her husband. Then the princess answered him and said, "I thank you, dear father; if you see the Green Knight, greet him and tell him that I am waiting and longing for him, for he alone and no other can free me from my suffering."

When the princess said that, she was thinking of the green churchyard with its many green mounds, for she longed for death. But the king did not understand her and wondered much at the strange greeting to a strange knight whose name he had never heard of before; but he was accustomed to grant her every wish, so he only said he would not forget to greet the knight as soon as he met him. Then he bade his daughter a tender farewell and started on his journey to the meeting of the kings.

There he found many princes, young nobles and knights, but among them there was no one called the Green Knight, so that the king could not deliver his daughter's message. At last he started on his homeward journey and had to cross high mountains and wide rivers and to go through dense forests. And as the king one day was passing through one of those great woods with his train, they came upon a large open space where thousands of boars were feeding. These were not wild, but tame, and were guarded by a swineherd in the garb of a huntsman who sat, surrounded by his dogs, on a little knoll and had a pipe to whose notes all animals listened and were obedient.

The king wondered at this herd of tame boars, and had one of his retainers ask the swineherd to whom they belonged. He answered that they belonged to the Green Knight. Then the king remembered what his daughter had asked him, and he himself rode up to the man and asked whether the Green Knight lived in the neighborhood.

"No," he replied, "he lives far from here, towards the east. If you ride in that direction you will meet other herdsmen who will show you the way to his castle."

Then the king and his men rode eastward for three days through a great forest, until they came again to a large plain surrounded by great forests, on which immense herds of elks and wild oxen were grazing. These also were guarded by a herdsman in hunter's dress, accompanied by his dogs. And the king rode to the man, who told him that all these herds belonged to the Green Knight, who lived further eastward. And again after three days the King came to a great clearing, where he saw great herds of stags and does, and the herdsman, in answer to his question, said that the Green Knight's castle was but a day's journey distant. Then the king rode for a day on green paths, through green woods, until he came to a great castle which was also green, for it was entirely covered by vines and climbing plants. When they rode up to the castle, a large number of men dressed in green like hunters, appeared and escorted them into the castle, and announced that the king of such and such a kingdom had arrived and desired to greet their master. Then the lord of the castle came himself -- a tall, handsome, young man, also clad in green -- and bade his guest welcome and entertained them in a lordly manner.

Then said the king, "You live far away and you have so great a domain that I had to go much out of my way to fulfill my daughter's wish. When I rode forth to attend the gathering of the kings, she asked me to greet the Green Knight for her, and to tell him how she longed for him, and that he alone could free her from her torment. This is a very strange commission that I have undertaken, but my daughter knows what is right and proper, and moreover I promised her mother on her deathbed that I would never refuse our only child a wish; so I have come here to deliver the message and keep my promise."

Then the Green Knight said to the king, "Your daughter was sad, and was certainly not thinking of me when she gave you her message, for she can never have heard of me; she was probably thinking of the churchyard with its many green mounds, where alone she hoped to find rest. But perhaps I can give her something to alleviate her sorrow. Take this little book, and tell the princess when she is sad and heavy-hearted to open her east window and to read in the book; it will gladden her heart."

Then the knight gave the king a little green book, but he could not read it, because he did not know the letters with which the words were written. He took it, however, and thanked the Green Knight for his kind and hospitable reception. He was very sorry, he assured the knight, that he had disturbed him, as the princess had not meant him at all.

They had to remain overnight in the castle, and the knight would gladly have kept them longer, but the king insisted that he must leave the next day; so the following morning he said goodbye to his host, and rode back the way he had come until he came to the clearing where the boars were, and from there he went straight home.

The first thing the king did, was to go to the island and take the little green book to his daughter. She was astonished when her father told her about the Green Knight, and gave her his greetings and the book, for she had not thought of a human being, nor had she the faintest idea that a Green Knight existed. But that very evening, when her father was gone, the princess opened her east window and began to read her green book, although it was not written in her mother tongue. The book contained many poems, and its language was beautiful. One of the first things that she read began as follows:

The wind has risen on the sea,
And bloweth over field and lea,

And while on earth broods silent night,
Who, to the knight, her troth will plight?

While she was reading the first verse she heard distinctly the rushing of the wind over the water; at the second verse she heard a rustling in the trees; at the third verse her ladies in waiting and all those in or near the palace, fell into a deep slumber. And when the princess read the fourth line, the Green Knight himself flew through the window in the shape of a bird.

Then he resumed his human form, greeted her kindly, and begged her to have no fear. The knight told her that he was the Green Knight whom the king had visited, and from whom he had received the book, and that she herself had brought him thither by reading those lines. She could speak freely to him, and this would relieve her sadness. Then the princess at once felt a great confidence in him, so that she told him her inmost thoughts; and the knight spoke to her with such sympathy and understanding that she felt happy as never before.

Then he said to her that every time she opened the book and read those first verses, the same would come to pass that had happened that evening; everybody on the island would fall asleep except the princess, and he would come to her immediately, although he lived far from her. And the prince also told her that he would always gladly come to her if she really wanted to see him. Now, however, she would better close the book and betake herself to rest.

And at the very moment that she closed the book, the Green Knight disappeared, and the court ladies and all the attendants awoke. Then the princess went to bed and dreamed of the knight and all that he had said to her. When she awoke the next morning she was light-hearted and happy as she had never been before, and day by day her health improved. Her cheeks grew rosy and she laughed and jested, so that all about her were amazed at the change that had taken place in her.

The king said that the evening air and the little green book had really helped her, and the princess agreed with him. But what nobody knew was, that every evening when the princess had read in her book, she received a visit from the Green Knight, and that they had long talks together. On the third visit he gave her a gold ring, and they became betrothed. But not until three months had elapsed could he go to her father and ask her hand in marriage; then he would take her home with him as his beloved wife.

In the meantime the stepmother learned that the princess was growing stronger and more beautiful, and that she was happier than ever before. The queen wondered at this and was vexed, for she had always believed and hoped that the princess would waste away and die, and that then her own daughter would become princess and heiress to the throne.

So one day she sent one of her court ladies over to the island to pay the princess a visit, and to try to find out what was the cause of this remarkable improvement. On the following day the young woman returned and told the queen that it seemed to be particularly helpful to the princess to sit at an open window every evening and read in a book that a strange prince had given her. The evening air had made her drowsy and she had fallen into a deep sleep; the same thing, she said, happened every evening to the court ladies who complained that it made them ill, while the princess became rosier and happier every day. The next day the queen sent her daughter to act as a spy, and told her to pay careful attention to all that the princess did.

"There is some mystery about that window; perhaps a man comes in by it."

The daughter came back the next day, but she could not tell any more than the maid, for she, too, had fallen into a deep sleep when the princess seated herself at the window and began to read.

Then on the third day the stepmother went herself to call on the princess. She was as sweet as honey to her, and pretended to be delighted to see how well she was. The queen questioned her as much as she dared, but could learn nothing from her. Then she went to the east window where the princess was in the habit of sitting and reading every evening, and examined it carefully, but could discover nothing special about it. The window was high above the ground, but vines grew up to it, so that it might have been possible for a very active person to climb up. For that reason the queen took a small pair of scissors, smeared them with poison, and fastened them in the window with their points turned upward, but in such a manner that no one could see them. When evening came and the princess seated herself at the window with the little green book in her hand, the queen said to herself that she would take good care not to fall asleep as the others had done. But her resolve did not help her in the least, for, in spite of herself, when the princess began to read, the queen's eyelids fell and she slept soundly as did the others. And at that same moment the Green Knight in the form of a bird came in through the window, unseen and unheard by all except the princess. They talked of their love for each other and how there remained only one week of the three months, and then the knight would go to her father's court and ask for her hand in marriage. Then he would take her home, and she would always be with him in his green castle, which lay in the midst of the great woodland realm over which he ruled, and about which he had told her so often.

Then the Green Knight bade his betrothed a tender farewell, resumed the form of a bird, and flew out of the window. But he flew so low that he grazed the scissors that the queen had fastened there, and scratched one leg.

He uttered a cry, but disappeared quickly. The princess, who had heard him, sprang up; but in so doing, the book fell from her hand to the floor and closed, and she also uttered a piercing cry which awoke the queen and all the court ladies. They rushed to her and asked what had happened. She answered that nothing was the matter, but that she had only dozed a little, and had been awakened by a bad dream. But that very hour she became ill with a fever and had to go to bed at once. The queen, in the meantime, slipped to the window to get her scissors, and when she found that there was blood on them, she hid them under her apron and took them home.

The princess, however, could not sleep the whole night, and felt miserable all the next day; nevertheless towards evening she rose in order to get a little fresh air. So she seated herself at the open east window, opened the book and read as usual:

The wind has risen on the sea,
And bloweth over field and lea,
And while on earth broods silent night
Who to the knight her troth will plight?

And the wind soughed through the trees, and the leaves rustled and all slept, except the princess -- but the knight came not. And so the days passed and she waited and watched, and read in her little green book and sang -- but no Green Knight came. Then her red cheeks again became pale and her happy heart, sad and heavy; and she began to waste away, to the sorrow of her father, but to the secret joy of her stepmother.

One day the princess walked feebly alone through the castle garden on the island, and seated herself on a bench under a high tree, and there she remained a long time plunged in sad and gloomy thoughts; while she was there two ravens came and perched on a branch over her head, and began to talk together.

"It is pitiful," said one, "to see our dear princess grieving to death for her beloved."

"Yes," said the other one, "especially as she is the only one who can cure him of the wound inflicted on him by the poisoned scissors of the queen."

"How so?" asked the first raven.

"Like cures like," replied the other one. "Over yonder, in the courtyard of the king, west of the stables, there lies, in a hole under a stone, an adder with her nine young. If the princess could get these and cook them, and give three young adders every day to the sick knight, he would recover. Otherwise there is no help for him."

As soon as night came the princess slipped out of the castle, went down to the shore where she found a boat, and rowed over to the palace. She went straight to the stone in the courtyard and rolled it away, heavy as it was, and there she found the nine young adders. These she tied up in her apron, and went forth on the way that she knew her father had taken when he returned from the gathering of the kings.

So she traveled on foot for weeks and months over high mountains and through dense forests, until she came at last upon the same swineherd that her father had met. He pointed out to her the way through the woods to the second herdsman, who in turn showed her the path to the third man. At last she reached the green castle where the knight lived, and lay sick with the poison and a fever, so ill that he recognized nobody, but only rolled and tossed in anguish and pain. Physicians had been called from the ends of the earth, but no one could procure for him the slightest relief.

The princess went into the kitchen and asked whether they could not give her some employment; she would wash the dishes, or do anything they asked her to, if only they would allow her to stay. The cook consented, and because she was so neat and quick and willing at every kind of work, he soon found her a valuable helper, and let her have her own way in many things.

So one day she said to him, "Today you must let me prepare the soup for our sick master. I know very well how it ought to be cooked, but I want to be allowed to cook it alone, and no one may look into the pot."

The cook was willing, and so she cooked three of the young adders in the soup, which was carried up to the Green Knight. And when he had eaten the soup, the fever went down so much that he could recognize those about him and speak intelligently; then he called the cook, and asked him whether he had cooked the soup that had done him so much good. The cook answered that he had done so, as no one else was allowed to prepare the food for his master. Then the Green Knight bade him make more of the same kind of soup on the morrow.

Now it was the cook's turn to go to the princess and beg her to prepare the soup for the knight; and as before, she cooked three young adders in it. This time, after partaking of it, he felt so well that he could get up out of bed. At this, all the doctors were amazed and could not understand how it happened; but, of course, they said that the medicines they had been giving him were beginning to have an effect.

On the third day, the kitchen maid again had to prepare the soup, and she cooked in it the last three young adders. And as soon as the knight had eaten it he felt perfectly well. Then he jumped up and wanted to go down to the kitchen himself to thank the cook, for, after all, he was certainly the best physician.

Now it happened that when he entered the kitchen there was no one there except a maid who was wiping dishes; but even as he looked he recognized her, and it suddenly dawned upon him what she had done for him. He folded her in his arms and said, "It was you then, was it not, who saved my life and cured me of the poison that penetrated into my blood, when I scratched myself on the scissors that the queen had put into the window?" She could not deny it; she was overjoyed, and he also. Soon after that their wedding was celebrated in the green castle; and there they are probably still living together and ruling over all the inhabitants of the green forests.

The Cinder Maid by Joseph Jacobs

Once upon a time, though it was not in my time or in your time, or in anybody else's time, there was a great king who had an only son, the prince and heir who was about to come of age. So the king sent round a herald who should blow his trumpet at every four corners where two roads met. And when the people came together he would call out, "O yes, O yes, O yes, know ye that his grace the king will give on Monday sennight" -- that meant seven nights or a week after -- "a royal ball to which all maidens of noble birth are hereby summoned; and be it furthermore known unto you that at this ball his highness the prince will select unto himself a lady that shall be his bride and our future queen. God save the king."

Now there was among the nobles of the king's court one who had married twice, and by the first marriage he had but one daughter, and as she was growing up her father thought that she ought to have someone to look after her. So he married again, a lady with two daughters, and his new wife, instead of caring for his daughter, thought only of her own and favored them in every way. She would give them beautiful dresses but none to her stepdaughter who had only to wear the castoff clothes of the other two. The noble's daughter was set to do all the drudgery of the house, to attend the kitchen fire, and had naught to sleep on but the heap of cinder raked out in the scullery; and that is why they called her Cinder Maid. And no one took pity on her and she would go and weep at her mother's grave where she had planted a hazel tree, under which she sat.

You can imagine how excited they all were when they heard the king's proclamation called out by the herald. "What shall we wear, mother; what shall we wear?" cried out the two daughters, and they all began talking about which dress should suit the one and what dress should suit the other, but when the father suggested that Cinder Maid should also have a dress they all cried out, "What, Cinder Maid going to the king's ball? Why, look at her, she would only disgrace us all." And so her father held his peace.

Now when the night came for the royal ball Cinder Maid had to help the two sisters to dress in their fine dresses and saw them drive off in the carriage with her father and their mother. But she went to her own mother's grave and sat beneath the hazel tree and wept and cried out:

Tree o' mine, O tree o' me,

With my tears I've watered thee;
Make me a lady fair to see,
Dress me as splendid as can be.
And with that the little bird on the tree called out to her:
Cinder Maid, Cinder Maid, shake the tree,
Open the first nut that you see.

So Cinder Maid shook the tree and the first nut that fell she took up and opened, and what do you think she saw? -- a beautiful silk dress blue as the heavens, all embroidered with stars, and two little lovely shoon [shoes] made of shining copper. And when she had dressed herself the hazel tree opened and from it came a coach all made of copper with four milk-white horses, with coachman and footmen all complete. And as she drove away the little bird called out to her:

Be home, be home ere mid-o'-night
Or else again you'll be a fright.

When Cinder Maid entered the ballroom she was the loveliest of all the ladies, and the prince, who had been dancing with her stepsisters, would only dance with her. But as it came towards midnight Cinder Maid remembered what the little bird had told her and slipped away to her carriage. And when the prince missed her he went to the guards at the palace door and told them to follow the carriage. But Cinder Maid when she saw this, called out:

Mist behind and light before,
Guide me to my father's door.

And when the prince's soldiers tried to follow her there came such a mist that they couldn't see their hands before their faces. So they couldn't find which way Cinder Maid went.

When her father and stepmother and two sisters came home after the ball they could talk of nothing but the lovely lady: "Ah, would not you have like to have been there?" said the sisters to Cinder Maid as she helped them to take off their fine dresses. "The was a most lovely lady with a dress like the heavens and shoes of bright copper, and the prince would dance with none but her; and when midnight came she disappeared and the prince could not find her. He is going to give a second ball in the hope that she will come again. Perhaps she will not, and then we will have our chance."

When the time of the second royal ball came round the same thing happened as before; the sisters teased Cinder Maid, saying "Wouldn't you like to come with us?" and drove off again as before.

And Cinder Maid went again to the hazel tree over her mother's grave and cried:

Tree o' mine, O tree o' me,
Shiver and shake, dear little tree;
Make me a lady fair to see,
Dress me as splendid as can be.
And then the little bird on the tree called out:
Cinder Maid, Cinder Maid, shake the tree,
Open the first nut that you see.

But this time she found a dress all golden brown like the earth embroidered with flowers, and her shoon were made of silver; and when the carriage came from the tree, lo and behold, that was made of silver too, drawn by black horses with trappings all of silver, and the lace on the coachman's and footmen's liveries was also of silver; and when Cinder Maid went to the ball the prince would dance with none but her; and when midnight came round she fled as before. But the prince, hoping to prevent her running away, had ordered the soldiers at the foot of the staircase to pour out honey on the stairs so that her shoes would stick in it. But Cinder Maid leaped from stair to stair and got away just in time, calling out as the soldiers tried to follow her:

Mist behind and light before,
Guide me to my father's door.

And when her sisters got home they told her once more of the beautiful lady that had come in a silver coach and silver shoon and in a dress all embroidered with flowers: "Ah, wouldn't you have like to have been there?" said they.

Once again the prince gave a great ball in the hope that his unknown beauty would come to it. All happened as before; as soon as the sisters had gone Cinder Maid went to the hazel tree over her mother's grave and called out:

Tree o' mine, O tree o' me,
Shiver and shake, dear little tree;
Make me a lady fair to see,

Dress me as splendid as can be.
And then the little bird appeared and said:
Cinder Maid, Cinder Maid, shake the tree,
Open the first nut that you see.

And when she opened the nut in it was a dress of silk green as the sea
with waves upon it, and her shoes this time were made of gold; and when
the coach came out of the tree it was also made of gold, with gold trappings
for the horses and for the retainers. And as she drove off the little bird from
the tree called out:

Be home, be home ere mid-o'-night
Or else again you'll be a fright.

Now this time, when Cinder Maid came to the ball, she was a desirous
to dance only with the prince as he with her, and so, when midnight came
round, she had forgotten to leave till the clock began to strike, one -- two --
three -- four -- five -- six, -- and then she began to run away down the stairs
as the clock struck eight -- nine -- ten. But the prince had told his soldier to
put tar upon the lower steps of the stairs; and as the clock struck eleven her
shoes stuck in the tar, and when she jumped to the foot of the stairs one of
her golden shoes was left behind, and just then the clock struck TWELVE,
and the golden coach with its horses and footmen, disappeared, and the
beautiful dress of Cinder Maid changed again into her ragged clothes and
she had to run home with only one golden shoe.

You can imagine how excited the sister were when they came home
and told Cinder Maid all about it, how that the beautiful lady had come in a
golden coach in a dress like the sea, with golden shoes, and how all had disappeared at midnight except the golden shoe. "Ah, wouldn't you have liked
to have been there?" said they.

Now when the prince found out that he could not keep his lady-love nor
trace where she had gone he spoke to his father and showed him the golden
shoe, and told him that he would never marry anyone but the maiden who
could wear that shoe. So the king, his father, ordered the herald to take
round the golden shoe upon a velvet cushion and to go to every four corners
where two streets met and sound the trumpet and call out, "O yes, O yes, O
yes, be it known unto you all that whatsoever lady of noble birth can fit this
shoe upon her foot shall become the bride of his highness the prince and our
future queen. God save the king."

And when the herald came to the house of Cinder Maid's father the eldest of her two stepsisters tried on the golden shoe, But it was much too small

for her, as it was for every other lady that had tried it up to that time; but she went up into her room and with a sharp knife cut off one of her toes and part of her heel, and then fitted her foot into the shoe, and when she came down she shoed it to the herald, who sent a message to the palace saying that the lady had been found who could wear the golden shoe.

Thereupon the prince jumped at once upon his horse and rode to the house of Cinder Maid's father. But when he saw the stepsister with the golden shoe, "Ah," he said, "but this is not the lady."

"But," she said, "you promised to marry the one that could wear the golden shoe," And the prince could say nothing, but offered to take her on his horse to his father's palace, for in those days ladies used to ride on a pillion at the back of the gentleman riding on horseback.

Now as they were riding towards the palace her foot began to drip with blood, and the little bird from the hazel tree that had followed them called out:

Turn and peep, turn and peep,
There's blood within the shoe;
A bit is cut from off the heel
And a bit from off the toe.

And the prince looked down and saw the blood streaming from her shoe and then he knew that this was not his true bride, and he rode back to the house of Cinder Maid's father; and then the second sister tried her chance; but when she found that her foot wouldn't fit the shoe she did the same as her sister, but all happed as before. The little bird called out:

Turn and peep, turn and peep,
There's blood within the shoe;
A bit is cut from off the heel
And a bit from off the toe.

And the prince took her back to her mother's house, and then he asked, "Have you no other daughter?" and the sisters cried out, "No, sir."

But the father said, "Yes, I have another daughter.

And the sisters cried out, "Cinder Maid, Cinder Maid, she could not wear that shoe."

But the prince said, "As she is of noble birth she has a right to try the shoe." So the herald went down to the kitchen and found cinder Maid; and when she saw her golden shoe she took it from him and put it on her foot,

which it fitted exactly; and then she took the other golden shoe from underneath the cinders where she had hidden it and put that on too.

Then the herald knew that she was the true bride of his master; and her
took her upstairs to where the prince was; when he saw her face, he knew
that she was the lady of his love. So he took her behind him upon his horse;
and as they rode to the palace the little bird from the hazel tree cried out:

Some cut their heel, and some cut their toe,

But she sat by the fire who could wear the shoe.

And so they were married and lived happy ever afterwards.

Little Gold Star by Unknown

(Spanish Oral Tradition)

Once upon a time, in what is now New Mexico, there lived a kind shepherd and his little girl, Teresa. She tended the house while he minded the sheep, and together they lived happily. Until one day, a neighbor lady began to coming to visit.

Soon, she was suggesting they marry, saying that he must be as lonely as she, a widow. But Tomás the shepherd did not want to marry her. That's when the widow started crying, and now Tomás felt that he must marry her. So he did. No sooner had she moved in with her daughters, Isabel and Inez, than she became cold and cruel to Tomás' girl.

Poor little Teresa had to do all the chores. Now her father went to market one day, and brought gifts back for the family. For the stepdaughters and their mother, gifts of flowers and oranges. To Teresa, he gave a lamb with soft white fleece. As soon as her husband returned to his flocks, Teresa's stepmother killed the lamb.

Handing the heartbroken girl the fleece, she ordered, "Go wash this in the river so I can make myself a soft pillow." So Teresa ran to the river and tried to wash the fleece, but a fish jumped up, grabbed it and swam away. That's when she heard a woman's voice asking her, "Why are you crying?" And the girl told her why, and the woman, who was wearing a blue gown and shawl, with gold edging, said, "Go up to that little shack on the mountainside. Tend the old man and the child there, and sweep the floor, and I will bring the fleece back to you. "So the girl went to the hut, where a baby wailed in his cradle, and an old man with long, tangled hair snored by the fire. She rocked the baby and sang to him while she combed the old man's hair. Then she swept, and the woman returned.

"Good child, your kindness carries its own blessing." She touched Teresa's forehead with her finger and a little gold star appeared there. Teresa did not know it, but the woman was Blessed Mary. The old man was Saint Joseph, and the baby was the Holy Child, the Baby Jesus.

Now Teresa ran home with the snow white fleece, but all she got was a beating. Her stepmother grabbed the fleece from her: it turned muddy brown. So she sent her own daughter, Isabel, to the river to wash it the next day. That's where the woman in blue found her, screaming at the fish who had just carried the fleece away. She told the girl to tend the old man and the baby and to take the stewpot off the fire. In return, she would restore the fleece. But inside the shack, Isabel spanked the Holy Infant because he was crying, pulled Saint Joseph's beard, and dropped the pot, spilling stew all over the floor. When Blessed Mary returned, she gave Isabel the now-spotless fleece. But, as she touched the girl's forehead, she said, "Your unkindness carries its own penance."

At this, horns grew out of the sides of Isabel's head. Her mother was furious when she saw them, and but the harder she pulled on them, the longer they grew, and the dirtier the fleece became!

The next day, Inez must have her turn to clean the fleece. The same fish grabbed it for the third time, and for the third time Blessed Mary appeared. She sent Inez to the hut and the girl scolded the Holy Infant, ignored Saint Joseph, and strewed the hearth ashes all over the floor. For her punishment, the girl sprouted a pair of donkey's ears. All her mother could do when she got home was to cover them up with a black mantilla. Now Teresa's life became much worse.

Her stepsisters jeered at her all the time, mocking her for the star out of shame for their own ugliness. Soon, the day to honor the patron saint of the town came, and there was a big fiesta planned. Early that morning, Teresa and her family went to church. While there, Don Miguel, the rich man who whose mansion overlooked the plaza noticed the girl with the star on her forehead. When church was over, Teresa was sent home to clean and cook, while her sisters went on to the plaza. Later that night, Don Miguel invited all to come to his home to celebrate. Isabel and Inez went with their mother in a carriage, but Teresa walked alone.

She sipped refreshments in the plaza, and danced with Don Miguel when he asked her to. But now her hateful stepmother recognized her, and Teresa fled before she was beaten again. Poor Don Miguel! Where had the girl gone? He looked all over the plaza, but she was gone. The next day, Don Miguel visited each house in the village. He was determined to find that girl! At Teresa's, the step sisters each tried to outdo the other with their hospitality. They brought hot chocolate and little cakes which they had made, but Don Miguel would not catch their eyes. Meanwhile, Teresa's stepmother had locked her into her bedroom. All she could do was to sit and listen. That's when she heard the cat say, "Narow, narow! Little Gold Star is here, right in the house!"

And so Don Miguel insisted that he see her. He at once asked her to marry him, but Teresa knew that she would need permission from her stepmother to do so. And the woman told her, "You must do three things before we return from the market. If you fail, I will refuse Don Miguel's marriage offer." "First, you must fill ten bottles with birds' tears," said one sister.

"Next, you must stuff twelve mattresses with birds' feathers," said the other. "Finally," said the stepmother, "you must prepare a tableful of fine food." And with that, they left her alone. Teresa did the best she could. She gathered a few grains of rice and some beans from the cabinets, but there were no birds anywhere that she could see. "Suddenly, there was a tap on the door. Blessed Mary stood there. "Do not worry," she said. "Touch your gold star and call the birds of heaven to help."

Teresa did, and instantly, the sky was filled with birds. They wept until she filled ten bottles with their tears. The second time she touched her star, the birds shed feathers like soft rain, while Teresa stuffed twelve mattresses. When she touched the star a third time, the birds flew away and came back, carry delicacies of every sort.

Now her stepmother knew that Teresa had been blessed. The whole village rejoiced, and gradually Teresa's stepmother grew less disagreeable and began to treat her as a daughter. Isabel and Inez grew kinder, and the donkey ears and horns became smaller then finally disappeared. Miguel and Teresa lived lovingly all their days. And the little gold star remained a sign of heaven's blessing on them and their children.

Kongji and Patzzi by Unknown

(Korean Oral Tradition)

A childless couple was granted with a very beautiful baby girl whom they named Kongji. Her mother died when Kongji was 100 days old. She grew up with her father. The man remarried again when Kongji was fourteen years old. To replace his wife, he found a cruel widow who had a very ugly daughter named Patzzi. Her father died eventually. From that time onwards, the stepmother and Patzzi treated Kongji very unfairly. They starved her, dressed her in rags and forced her to do all the dirtiest work in the house.

One day, the stepmother forced Kongji to plow a field with a wooden hoe. The hoe soon broke, leaving Kongji in tears, for fear that her stepmother would beat her again. A cow appeared and comforted her. He plowed the field in her place, and sent Kongji home with a basket of apples, a gift from the cow. Her stepmother accused her of stealing the apples and gave the entire basket to Patzzi. And she refused to give Kongji her supper.

The next day, the stepmother gave Kongji enormous pot with a hole in the bottom. She has to fill it with water before she and Patzzi return home from town. Kongji kept bringing baskets of water but the pot was never filled. The water leaked out from the hole. A turtle appeared and blocked the hole for her. With his help, Kongji filled the pot with water. The stepmother was even angrier. She spanked Kongji black and blue.

After a time, the King announced that he was looking for a wife. A dance will be given in his honor, to which every maiden must attend. Kongji and Patzzi were invited. The stepmother was hopeful that Patzzi would be the lucky one, but was afraid that Kongji would spoil her own daughter's chance. Before they left, the stepmother gave Kongji a huge sack of rice to clean, which she must accomplish before they return from the dance. Kongji asked for help from the heavens, and a flock of sparrows appeared and hulled the rice. A fairy came down from heaven and dressed Kongji in a beautiful gown and a delicate pair of colorful shoes. She was transported to the palace by four men in a magnificent palanquin. Kongji hurried towards the dance.

Everyone admired her because of her beauty. The King went to her to ask her name. But when Kongji saw her stepmother and stepsister among the guests, she fled with terror. Patzzi remarked to her mother that the strange girl looks like her Kongji. As Kongji crossed a bridge, she tripped. One of her shoes fell into the stream. The King found the shoe and vowed to marry the woman it belonged to. Servants tried the shoe on every woman in the land, until they arrived in Kongji's village. It fits no one, only Kongji. She was the last to try the shoe. Then she produced her clothes and the other pair of her shoes. The King and Kongji were married.

Patzzi was jealous of Kongji's marriage and drowned her in a river. Patzzi disguised herself as Kongji to live with the King. Kongji's spirit would haunt anyone in the river. A brave man confronted her ghost and she told him everything. The man reported this to the King, and the King went into the river. Instead of a dead body, he retrieved a golden lotus. He kissed the lotus and it was changed back into Kongji.

The King sentenced Patzzi to death and had the servants make sauce from her body. They sent it to the stepmother. The stepmother ate the sauce greedily, mistaking it as a gift from her daughter. A cock revealed to her everything. When she learned of Patzzi's death, Kongji's stepmother fell in a faint from which she never awoke.

The Girl with the Rose Red Slippers by Aesop

IN the last days of Ancient Egypt, not many years before the country was conquered by the Persians, she was ruled by a Pharaoh called Amasis. So as to strengthen his country against the threat of invasion by Cyrus of Persia, who was conquering all the known world, he welcomed as many Greeks as wished to trade with or settle in Egypt, and gave them a city called Naucratis to be entirely their own.

In Naucratis, not far from the mouth of the Nile that flows into the sea at Canopus, there lived a wealthy Greek merchant called Charaxos. His true home was in the island of Lesbos, and the famous poetess Sappho was his sister; but he had spent most of his life trading with Egypt, and in his old age he settled at Naucratis.

One day when he was walking in the marketplace he saw a great crowd gathered round the place where the slaves were sold. Out of curiosity he pushed his way into their midst, and found that everyone was looking at a beautiful girl who had just been set up on the stone rostrum to be sold.

She was obviously a Greek with white skin and cheeks like blushing roses, and Charaxos caught his breath - for he had never seen anyone so lovely.

Consequently, when the bidding began, Charaxos determined to buy her and, being one of the wealthiest merchants in all Naucratis, he did so without much difficulty.

When he had bought the girl, he discovered that her name was Rhodopis and that she had been carried away by pirates from her home in the north of Greece when she was a child. They had sold her to a rich man who employed many slaves on the island of Samos, and she had grown up there, one of her fellow slaves being an ugly little man called Aesop who was always kind to her and told her the most entrancing stories and fables about animals and birds and human beings.

But when she was grown up, her master wished to make some money out of so beautiful a girl and had sent her to rich Naucratis to be sold.

Charaxos listened to her tale and pitied her deeply. Indeed very soon he became quite besotted about her. He gave her a lovely house to live in, with a garden in the middle of it, and slave girls to attend on her. He heaped her with presents of jewels and beautiful clothes, and spoiled her as if she had been his own daughter.

One day a strange thing happened as Rhodopis was bathing in the marble-edged pool in her secret garden. The slave-girls were holding her clothes and guarding her jeweled girdle and her rose-red slippers of which she was particularly proud, while she lazed in the cool water - for a summer's day even in the north of Egypt grows very hot about noon.

Suddenly when all seemed quiet and peaceful, an eagle came swooping down out of the clear blue sky, down, straight down as if to attack the little group by the pool. The slave-girls dropped everything they were holding and fled shrieking to hide among the trees and flowers of the garden; and Rhodopis rose from the water and stood with her back against the marble fountain at one end of it, gazing with wide, startled eyes.

But the eagle paid no attention to any of them. Instead, it swooped right down and picked up one of her rose-red slippers in its talons. Then it soared up into the air again on its great wings and, still carrying the slipper, flew away to the south over the valley of the Nile.

Rhodopis wept at the loss of her rose-red slipper, feeling sure that she would never see it again, and sorry also to have lost anything that Charaxos had given to her.

But the eagle seemed to have been sent by the gods - perhaps by Horus himself whose sacred bird he was. For he flew straight up the Nile to Memphis and then swooped, down towards the palace.

At that hour Pharaoh Amasis sat in the great courtyard doing justice to his people and hearing any complaints that they wished to bring.

Down over the courtyard swooped the eagle and dropped the rose-red slipper of Rhodopis into Pharaoh's lap.

The people cried out in surprise when they saw, this, and Amasis too was much taken aback. But, as he took up the little rose-red slipper and admired the delicate workmanship and the tiny size of it, he felt that the girl for whose foot it was made must indeed be one of the loveliest in the world.

Indeed Amasis the Pharaoh was so moved by what had happened that he issued a decree:

"Let my messengers go forth through all the cities of the Delta and, if need be, into Upper Egypt to the very borders of my kingdom. Let them take with them this rose-red slipper which the divine bird of Horus has brought to me, and let them declare that her from whose foot this slipper came shall be the bride of Pharaoh!"

Then the messengers prostrated themselves crying, 'Life, health, strength be to Pharaoh! Pharaoh has spoken and his command shall be obeyed!'

So they set forth from Memphis and went by way of Heliopolis and Tanis and Canopus until they came to Naucratis. Here they heard of the rich merchant Charaxos and of how he had bought the beautiful Greek girl in the slave market, and how he was lavishing all his wealth upon her as if she had been a princess put in his care by the gods.

So they went to the great house beside the Nile and found Rhodopis in the quiet garden beside the pool.

When they showed her the rose-red slipper she cried out in surprise that it was hers. She held out her foot so that they could see how well it fitted her; and she bade one of the slave girls fetch the pair to it which she had kept carefully in memory of her strange adventure with the eagle.

Then the messengers knew that this was the girl whom Pharaoh had sent them to find, and they knelt before her and said, 'The good god Pharaoh Amasis - life, health, strength be to him! - bids you come with all speed to his palace at Memphis. There you shall be treated with all honor and given a high place in his Royal House of Women: for he believes that Horus the son of Isis and Osiris sent that eagle to bring the rose-red slipper and cause him to search for you.'

Such a command could not be disobeyed. Rhodopis bade farewell to Charaxos, who was torn between joy at her good fortune and sorrow at his loss, and set out for Memphis.

And when Amasis saw her beauty, he was sure that the gods had sent her to him. He did not merely take her into his Royal House of Women, he made her his Queen and the Royal Lady of Egypt. And they lived happily together for the rest of their lives and died a year before the coming of Ambyses the Persian.

Bawang Putih and Bawang Merah by Unknown

(Indonesia)

ONCE upon a time, in East Java, lived a beautiful girl named Bawang Putih. Her father had died and she lived with her stepmother and stepsister. Before her father passed away, her stepmother and stepsister were very kind to her. But two days after the sad occurence, they began to treat her cruelly. Her stepmother said:

"Bawang Putih, from this moment, you have to clean the house, guard the house, wash the clothes, and cook all the meals."

"But mother…"

"No but! You must obey my rule! What do you think? I love you? I hate you! Why should I be kind to my stepdaughter?"

"How poor you are," said her stepsister with a sly smile.

Her stepsister was Bawang Merah. She was very lazy and wore beautiful clothes. But Bawang Putih was more beautiful than her and Bawang Merah knew this.

One day, Bawang Putih went to river to do the laundry. She heard a goldfish crying for help. Its mouth was hooked by an angler. Seeing the condition Bawang Putih felt sorry and helped it.

"Thank you for your kindness, would you like to be my friend?" asked the goldfish.

Bawang Putih was very surprised: the goldfish could speak! And Bawang Putih answered nervously: "Uh… Of course."

Then, the fish helped her in washing and they became best friends.

Unfortunately, their friendship couldn't last because her stepmother found out about it and ordered Bawang Merah to catch it. Bawang Merah caught the fish and gave it to her mother. After that, they cooked it, and ate it! Bawang Putih took the scaly bones of her golden friend and said:

"Oh my friend, forgive me… I didn't know they would eat you. I'm sorry I did not repay your kindness to me… Good bye friend, good bye…"

Bawang Putih buried her friend. Several days later, a beautiful tree grew from the fish's grave, with colorful blossom flowers. A Prince came to see it and needed the tree to help his father to be well again. The prince said:

"Who is the owner of the tree?"

"Oh, it's mine…" answered Bawang Merah.

"Could you give it to me?"

"Of course…"

Bawang Merah tried to pull it out but she couldn't. Everybody also tried, but none were strong enough. Then, the Prince looked at Bawang Putih and fell in love with her and asked her to uproot the tree. A miracle! The tree was removed from the ground and presented to the prince. The prince said:

"Oh beautiful girl. Thank you. I love you. Will you marry me?"

Bawang Putih smiled and nodded. The Prince married her, and Bawang Putih forgave her stepmother and stepsister. And they all lived happily ever after.

The Story of Tấm and Cám by Unknown

(Vietnam)

ONCE upon a time, in a village there was a family in which the wife died when her child, named Tấm, was still a small girl. Tấm's father soon married another woman and they had a daughter named Cám. The stepmother and Cám did not like Tấm and treated her badly. When Tấm's father died, the stepmother asked Tấm to do all the housework while she and her daughter did not do anything. Everyday Tấm had to work hard from dawn to dark.

One day, the stepmother told Tấm and Cám to fish. She promised that the one who caught more fish would get a red silk cloth called yếm to cover their belly. Tấm tried her best to get more and more fish while her stepsister, who was spoiled, did nothing. Cám ran around and even caught butterflies. At noon when they got ready to return home, Tấm held a basket full of fish while Cám still had an empty basket. Smiling beautifully, Cám told Tấm that Tấm's hair was covered by mud and had to wash it clean otherwise her stepmother would scold her for sure. While Tấm soaped her hair, Cám secretly put all the fish from Tấm's basket into her basket and ran home.

As Tấm finished, she did not see Cám anymore and knew what happened. She cried hard, knowing that her stepmother would say she was lazy and punish her. The Buddha showed up and asked her why she cried. Tấm told him her story. He told her to look at her basket to see if there was anything left. She found a little goby. The Buddha told her to take it home and put it into the well and taught her a poem to say when she came to feed it:

"Oh my dear little goby
Come here with me
Eat the golden rice,
the silver rice of me
Do not eat the stable rice of others."

After that, Tấm did as Buddha told her. She used a bowl of rice from her small food ration she got every day to feed the fish. Before feeding it, she always greeted it by the poem so the fish showed up. It became Tấm's best friend. The stepmother became curious about Tấm's behavior and said Cám to go after her. Cám found out that Tấm raised a goby and considered it as a friend. She told her mother. The following day, the stepmother told

Tấm to take their buffalos to a field which was far from their village. When she went away, the stepmother and Cám pretended to be Tấm to call the fish and caught it. They killed the fish and ate it.

In the evening, Tấm came home and she called and called four times but the fish did not show up. Tấm sobbed. The Buddha appeared and comforted her. He told Tấm to find the fish's bone and put it into four jars and bury each jar underneath a corner of her bed. Tấm tried to do this but she could not find the bones. She was so disappointed and cried again. A rooster said that if she gave him some rice, he would look for the fish bones for her. So Tấm gave him some rice and the rooster came into their kitchen, dug into the ash and found the fish's remains.

After a while, the king of the country held a big festival. Everyone was excited to come to the festival except Tấm. She did not have any new clothes to go while her stepmother and her stepsister had many beautiful dresses to wear. The stepmother also gave her a big bowl mixed of husked and white rice, told her to sort wash the rice before she went to the festival. While the stepmother and Cám was taking part in the festival, Tấm had to stay behind and do what the stepmother told her. She missed her mother so much. Her tears wetted her face. The Buddha came again and called sparrow that helped Tấm sort the rice. However Tấm still so sad because she could not go to the festival with such old clothes. The Buddha told her to take the four jars of fish bone up and in them she found very beautiful clothes, a pair of sparkling embroidered slippers, a saddle and a very beautiful white horse. Tấm wore the new clothes and new slippers, rode the horse to the festival. She looked stunning. No one who saw her could think of the poor girl she used to be. All people admired the beautiful lady.

On the way to the festival, she had to cross a puddle and dropped one of her slippers. A while after that, the King and his escort came by. The horse whinnied. The king told one of his servants to check the puddle and found the slipper of Tấm.

When the party started, the king proclaimed that he would marry the one whose foot fit the slipper. Every woman tried to put their foot into it but no one had any luck, including Cám and her mother. Finally, when Tấm put her foot into the slipper, the king knew he had found his queen. The king married Tấm and brought her into the Royal palace while her stepmother and Cám fumed. The king loved Tấm so much. Cám and her mother could not accept the idea that the beautiful queen was Tấm. The mother swore that she would make Cám's life be better than Tấm's.

When Tấm, now was the queen, came home for her father's death anniversary, the stepmother asked Tấm to climb an areca tree to pick some areca fruits to put on her father alter. While Tấm was on the top, the stepmother and Cám chopped the tree down so Tấm fell and died. The step-mother gave Tấm's clothes to Cám and brought Cám to the royal palace to take place of her stepsister. Tấm died, transferred into an oriole. The bird also flew to the palace.

The king missed Tấm dearly. All days he looked so sad although Cám tried her best to please him. One day, when Cám was washing the king's clothes, the oriole sang a song to say that she must wash the clothes carefully otherwise she would get punished. The king hears the bird singing and was so surprised that he told the bird that if it was his beloved wife, it should land on his sleeves. The bird did as his word. Since that time, the king went everywhere with the little bird. Cám grew jealous and told her mother about the oriole. Her mother told her to find a way to kill the bird. Cám strangled the oriole, ate it and burnt its feathers then threw the ashes into the garden.

At the place where the ash fell, a tree quickly grew. The king liked it and asked his servant to hang a hammock there for him. He would sleep in it and dream about Tấm. Cám got jealous again and told her mother about the tree. Her mother advised her to chop the tree down and use its wood to make a loom.

However, when Cám worked with the loom, she heard a voice told her that she stole Tấm's husband and would pay for what she did. Cám was terrified and ran to her mother for help. Her mother told her to burn the loom and throw its ashes far away from the palace.

At the place where she threw the ash of the loom, there rose a wonderful persimmon tree. It grew up magically and bore a fruit. An old woman walked on the road and saw the fruit. She smelled the sweet fragrance of the persimmons and begged for one. She promised to keep it, not to eat it. Amazingly, the fruit fell into her hand. The woman was happy to take it to her small hut. She lived alone, made her living by making tea and selling it to people. She kept her promise that she did not eat the fruit. She talked to it like a friend. The following day, when she came back from work, she was so surprised to see that her hut was very neat and clean. A hot meal was on the table waiting for her. The woman wondered who had been so kind to have helped her so much. Day after day, it happened again and again. The woman tried to find out who helped her so one day, she pretended to leave but stayed to see what would happen. Soon, she saw a very beautiful young woman, Tấm, walked from the fruit. Tấm started to do housework in the old woman's surprised eyes. The old woman came and quickly tore the peel fruit into pieces. Tấm could not come back to the fruit so she stayed with the old woman. The woman loved her and treated her like a dear daughter. Tấm prepared betels and areca nuts people chewing while they drank tea.

One day, the king stopped by their place. The old woman invited him to tea and betels. He could not believe in his eyes while seeing those special betels - they were shaped like phoenix wings which was the way Tấm used to make betels for him. The king asked the old woman who made those betels. The woman told him that her daughter had prepared them. The king wanted to meet her daughter. When he saw her, he realized it was his beloved wife and asked to bring her back to the palace. The king now loved her more than ever and they lived happily ever after.

Seeing Tấm return even much more beautiful than ever, Cám was furious with jealous rage. She asked Tấm how she could be so beautiful like that. Tấm told her that taking baths in boiling water had helped her. Cám jumped into a bath of boiling water and died.

Cám's body was then cut and put into a jar of food to send to her mother. The mother thought it was a kind of paste and enjoyed eating it, declaring it delicious. A crow standing on the roof of her house heard what she said and told her:

"Delicious? What is so delicious?

The mother is eating her daughter's flesh!

Is there anything left for me?"

The mother was angry and screamed at the black bird. The crow flew way, repeating its words. When the mother finally got to the bottom of the paste jar, she saw Cám's skull and died of shock.

Fair, Brown, and Trembling by Jeremiah Curtin

KING Aedh Cúrucha lived in Tir Conal, and he had three daughters, whose names were Fair, Brown, and Trembling.

Fair and Brown had new dresses, and went to church every Sunday. Trembling was kept at home to do the cooking and work. They would not let her go out of the house at all; for she was more beautiful than the other two, and they were in dread she might marry before themselves.

They carried on in this way for seven years. At the end of seven years the son of the king of Omanya [the ancient Emania in Ulster] fell in love with the eldest sister.

One Sunday morning, after the other two had gone to church, the old henwife came into the kitchen to Trembling, and said, "It's at church you ought to be this day, instead of working here at home."

"How could I go?" said Trembling. "I have no clothes good enough to wear at church; and if my sisters were to see me there, they'd kill me for going out of the house."

"I'll give you," said the henwife, "a finer dress than either of them has ever seen. And now tell me what dress will you have?"

"I'll have," said Trembling, "a dress as white as snow, and green shoes for my feet."

The henwife put on the cloak of darkness, clipped a piece from the old clothes the young woman had on, and asked for the whitest robes in the world and the most beautiful that could be found, and a pair of green shoes.

That moment she had the robe and the shoes, and she brought them to Trembling, who put them on. When Trembling was dressed and ready, the henwife said, "I have a honey-bird here to sit on your right shoulder, and a honey-finger to put on your left. At the door stands a milk-white mare, with a golden saddle for you to sit on, and a golden bridle to hold in your hand."

Trembling sat on the golden saddle; and when she was ready to start, the henwife said, "You must not go inside the door of the church, and the minute the people rise up at the end of mass, do you make off, and ride home as fast as the mare will carry you."

When Trembling came to the door of the church there was no one inside who could get a glimpse of her but was striving to know who she was; and when they saw her hurrying away at the end of mass, they ran out to overtake her. But no use in their running; she was away before any man could come near her. From the minute she left the church till she got home, she overtook the wind before her, and outstripped the wind behind.

She came down at the door, went in, and found the henwife had dinner ready. She put off the white robes, and had on her old dress in a twinkling.

When the two sisters came home the henwife asked, "Have you any news today from the church?"

"We have great news," said they. "We saw a wonderful, grand lady at the church door. The like of the robes she had we have never seen on woman before. It's little that was thought of our dresses beside what she had on; and there wasn't a man at the church, from the king to the beggar, but was trying to look at her and know who she was."

The sisters would give no peace till they had two dresses like the robes of the strange lady; but honey-birds and honey-fingers were not to be found.

Next Sunday the two sisters went to church again, and left the youngest at home to cook the dinner.

After they had gone, the henwife came in and asked, "Will you go to church today?"

"I would go," said Trembling, "if I could get the going."

"What robe will you wear?" asked the henwife.

"The finest black satin that can be found, and red shoes for my feet."

"What color do you want the mare to be?"

"I want her to be so black and so glossy that I can see myself in her body."

The henwife put on the cloak of darkness, and asked for the robes and the mare. That moment she had them. When Trembling was dressed, the henwife put the honey-bird on her right shoulder and the honey-finger on her left. The saddle on the mare was silver, and so was the bridle.

When Trembling sat in the saddle and was going away, the henwife ordered her strictly not to go inside the door of the church, but to rush away as soon as the people rose at the end of mass, and hurry home on the mare before any man could stop her.

That Sunday the people were more astonished than ever, and gazed at her more than the first time; and all they were thinking of was to know who she was. But they had no chance; for the moment the people rose at the end of mass she slipped from the church, was in the silver saddle, and home before a man could stop her or talk to her.

The henwife had the dinner ready. Trembling took off her satin robe, and had on her old clothes before her sisters got home.

"What news have you today?" asked the henwife of the sisters when they came from the church.

"Oh, we saw the grand strange lady again! And it's little that any man could think of our dresses after looking at the robes of satin that she had on! And all at church, from high to low, had their mouths open, gazing at her, and no man was looking at us."

The two sisters gave neither rest nor peace till they got dresses as nearly like the strange lady's robes as they could find. Of course they were not so good; for the like of those robes could not be found in Erin.

When the third Sunday came, Fair and Brown went to church dressed in black satin. They left Trembling at home to work in the kitchen, and told her to be sure and have dinner ready when they came back.

After they had gone and were out of sight, the henwife came to the kitchen and said, "Well, my dear, are you for church today?"

"I would go if I had a new dress to wear."

"I'll get you any dress you ask for. What dress would you like?" asked the henwife.

"A dress red as a rose from the waist down, and white as snow from the waist up; a cape of green on my shoulders; and a hat on my head with a red, a white, and a green feather in it; and shoes for my feet with the toes red, the middle white, and the backs and heels green."

The henwife put on the cloak of darkness, wished for all these things, and had them. When Trembling was dressed, the henwife put the honey-bird on her right shoulder and the honey-finger on her left, and placing the hat on her head, clipped a few hairs from one lock and a few from another with her scissors, and that moment the most beautiful golden hair was flowing down over the girl's shoulders. Then the henwife asked what kind of a mare she would ride. She said white, with blue and gold-colored diamond-shaped spots all over her body, on her back a saddle of gold, and on her head a golden bridle.

The mare stood there before the door, and a bird sitting between her ears, which began to sing as soon as Trembling was in the saddle, and never stopped till she came home from the church.

The fame of the beautiful strange lady had gone out through the world, and all the princes and great men that were in it came to church that Sunday, each one hoping that it was himself would have her home with him after mass.

The son of the king of Omanya forgot all about the eldest sister, and remained outside the church, so as to catch the strange lady before she could hurry away.

The church was more crowded than ever before, and there were three times as many outside. There was such a throng before the church that Trembling could only come inside the gate.

As soon as the people were rising at the end of mass, the lady slipped out through the gate, was in the golden saddle in an instant, and sweeping away ahead of the wind. But if she was, the prince of Omanya was at her side, and, seizing her by the foot, he ran with the mare for thirty perches, and never let go of the beautiful lady till the shoe was pulled from her foot, and he was left behind with it in his hand. She came home as fast as the mare could carry her, and was thinking all the time that the henwife would kill her for losing the shoe.

Seeing her so vexed and so changed in the face, the old woman asked, "What's the trouble that's on you now?"

"Oh! I've lost one of the shoes off my feet," said Trembling.

"Don't mind that; don't be vexed," said the henwife; "maybe it's the best thing that ever happened to you."

Then Trembling gave up all the things she had to the henwife, put on her old clothes, and went to work in the kitchen. When the sisters came home, the henwife asked, "Have you any news from the church?"

"We have indeed," said they; "for we saw the grandest sight today. The strange lady came again, in grander array than before. On herself and the horse she rode were the finest colors of the world, and between the ears of the horse was a bird which never stopped singing from the time she came till she went away. The lady herself is the most beautiful woman ever seen by man in Erin."

After Trembling had disappeared from the church, the son of the king of Omanya said to the other kings' sons, "I will have that lady for my own."

They all said, "You didn't win her just by taking the shoe off her foot, you'll have to win her by the point of the sword; you'll have to fight for her with us before you can call her your own."

"Well," said the son of the king of Omanya, "when I find the lady that shoe will fit, I'll fight for her, never fear, before I leave her to any of you."

Then all the kings' sons were uneasy, and anxious to know who was she that lost the shoe; and they began to travel all over Erin to know could they find her. The prince of Omanya and all the others went in a great company together, and made the round of Erin; they went everywhere -- north, south, east, and west. They visited every place where a woman was to be found, and left not a house in the kingdom they did not search, to know could they find the woman the shoe would fit, not caring whether she was rich or poor, of high or low degree.

The prince of Omanya always kept the shoe; and when the young women saw it, they had great hopes, for it was of proper size, neither large nor small, and it would beat any man to know of what material it was made. One thought it would fit her if she cut a little from her great toe; and another, with too short a foot, put something in the tip of her stocking. But no use, they only spoiled their feet, and were curing them for months afterwards.

The two sisters, Fair and Brown, heard that the princes of the world were looking all over Erin for the woman that could wear the shoe, and every day they were talking of trying it on; and one day Trembling spoke up and said, "Maybe it's my foot that the shoe will fit."

"Oh, the breaking of the dog's foot on you! Why say so when you were at home every Sunday?"

They were that way waiting, and scolding the younger sister, till the princes were near the place. The day they were to come, the sisters put Trembling in a closet, and locked the door on her. When the company came to the house, the prince of Omanya gave the shoe to the sisters. But though they tried and tried, it would fit neither of them.

"Is there any other young woman in the house?" asked the prince.

"There is," said Trembling, speaking up in the closet; "I'm here."

"Oh! we have her for nothing but to put out the ashes," said the sisters.

But the prince and the others wouldn't leave the house till they had seen her; so the two sisters had to open the door. When Trembling came out, the shoe was given to her, and it fitted exactly.

The prince of Omanya looked at her and said, "You are the woman the shoe fits, and you are the woman I took the shoe from."

Then Trembling spoke up, and said, "Do stay here till I return."

Then she went to the henwife's house. The old woman put on the cloak of darkness, got everything for her she had the first Sunday at church, and put her on the white mare in the same fashion. Then Trembling rode along the highway to the front of the house. All who saw her the first time said, "This is the lady we saw at church."

Then she went away a second time, and a second time came back on the black mare in the second dress which the henwife gave her. All who saw her the second Sunday said, "That is the lady we saw at church."

A third time she asked for a short absence, and soon came back on the third mare and in the third dress. All who saw her the third time said, "That is the lady we saw at church." Every man was satisfied, and knew that she was the woman.

Then all the princes and great men spoke up, and said to the son of the king of Omanya, "You'll have to fight now for her before we let her go with you."

"I'm here before you, ready for combat," answered the prince.

Then the son of the king of Lochlin stepped forth. The struggle began, and a terrible struggle it was. They fought for nine hours; and then the son of the king of Lochlin stopped, gave up his claim, and left the field. Next day the son of the king of Spain fought six hours, and yielded his claim. On the third day the son of the king of Nyerfó fought eight hours, and stopped. The fourth day the son of the king of Greece fought six hours, and stopped. On the fifth day no more strange princes wanted to fight; and all the sons of kings in Erin said they would not fight with a man of their own land, that the strangers had had their chance, and as no others came to claim the woman, she belonged of right to the son of the king of Omanya.

The marriage day was fixed, and the invitations were sent out. The wedding lasted for a year and a day. When the wedding was over, the king's son brought home the bride, and when the time came a son was born. The young woman sent for her eldest sister, Fair, to be with her and care for her.

One day, when trembling was well, and when her husband was away hunting, the two sisters went out to walk; and when they came to the seaside, the eldest pushed the youngest sister in. A great whale came and swallowed her.

The eldest sister came home alone, and the husband asked, "Where is your sister?"

"She has gone home to her father in Ballyshannon; now that I am well, I don't need her."

"Well," said the husband, looking at her, "I'm in dread it's my wife that has gone."

"Oh! no," said she; "it's my sister Fair that's gone."

Since the sisters were very much alike, the prince was in doubt. That night he put his sword between them, and said, "If you are my wife, this sword will get warm; if not, it will stay cold."

In the morning when he rose up, the sword was as cold as when he put it there.

It happened when the two sisters were walking by the seashore, that a little cowboy was down by the water minding cattle, and saw Fair push Trembling into the sea; and next day, when the tide came in, he saw the whale swim up and throw her out on the sand.

When she was on the sand she said to the cowboy, "When you go home in the evening with the cows, tell the master that my sister Fair pushed me into the sea yesterday; that a whale swallowed me, and then threw me out, but will come again and swallow me with the coming of the next tide; then he'll go out with the tide, and come again with tomorrow's tide, and throw me again on the strand. The whale will cast me out three times. I'm under the enchantment of this whale, and cannot leave the beach or escape myself. Unless my husband saves me before I'm swallowed the fourth time, I shall be lost. He must come and shoot the whale with a silver bullet when he turns on the broad of his back. Under the breast fin of the whale is a reddish-brown spot. My husband must hit him in that spot, for it is the only place in which he can be killed."

When the cowboy got home, the eldest sister gave him a draught of oblivion, and he did not tell.

Next day he went again to the sea. The whale came and cast Trembling on shore again. She asked the boy, "Did you tell the master what I told you to tell him?"

"I did not," said he; "I forgot."

"How did you forget?" asked she.

"The woman of the house gave me a drink that made me forget."

"Well, don't forget telling him this night; and if she gives you a drink, don't take it from her."

As soon as the cowboy came home, the eldest sister offered him a drink. He refused to take it till he had delivered his message and told all to the master.

The third day the prince went down with his gun and a silver bullet in it. He was not long down when the whale came and threw Trembling upon the beach as the two days before. She had no power to speak to her husband till he had killed the whale. Then the whale went out, turned over once on the broad of his back, and showed the spot for a moment only. That moment the prince fired. He had but the one chance, and a short one at that; but he took it, and hit the spot, and the whale, mad with pain, made the sea all around red with blood, and died.

That minute Trembling was able to speak, and went home with her husband, who sent word to her father what the eldest sister had done. The father came, and told him any death he chose to give her to give it. The prince told the father he would leave her life and death with himself. The father had her put out then on the sea in a barrel, with provisions in it for seven years.

In time Trembling had a second child, a daughter. The prince and she sent the cowboy to school, and trained him up as one of their own children, and said, "If the little girl that is born to us now lives, no other man in the world will get her but him."

The cowboy and the prince's daughter lived on till they were married. The mother said to her husband, "You could not have saved me from the whale but for the little cowboy; on that account I don't grudge him my daughter."

The son of the king of Omanya and Trembling had fourteen children, and they lived happily till the two died of old age.